MW01104366

Tangled in Motion

Tangled in Motion

Jane L. Carman

Journal of Experimental Fiction 62

jef

Dekalb, Illinois

Cover image: Leslie Raine Carman

ISBN-10   1-884097-63-4

ISBN-13   978-1-884097-63-8

ISSN   1084-547X

Journal of Experimental Fiction
The foremost in innovative fiction
Experimentalfiction.com

for the family I love

for seeing, believing, & hope

ACKNOWLEDGMENTS

Works presented in this collection have, in some, form appeared in the following journals:

580-Split
Cormac McCarthy's Dead Typewriter
Devil's Lake
Dirty : Dirty (Jaded Ibis Productions)
Elements
elimae
Festival Writer
Fiction Weekly
Heart Journal
Mixed Fruit
Pequin
Santa Clara Review
The Zepheyr

TABLE OF CONTENTS

TANGLED IN MOTION

Words give us the ability to move—Lidia Yuknavitch

All great works of literature either dissolve a genre or invent one—
Walter Benjamin

A sentence says that the end of it is that they send in order to better themselves in order to sentence—Gertrude Stein

U(n)/De(a)d/I(c)@-I-on

PREFACE: 100% C

1. C-a recipe
one part history
one part his   story
one part hi   story
one part his

one part her
one part

two parts secret
two parts scandal

three parts lie

half

baked

2. C-all about that curve

3. and gaping mouth

4. about a body working for a quarter a day

5. The Depression

6. the depression

7. the babies

8. one baby

9. the bastard baby that had to pay for his mother's   sins

amen
halleluiah
make a cross
all that jazz

10. the weather   whether

11. spinning

12. that twisted baby's insides out
that let the heart
flutter beyond its cage
let the intestines and intentions slither
past their walls spiraling
around the body
circling the legs and story
                    spinning it   a   way

14. about the souls free of mechanics

15. flaming prairies flashing orange against bruised skies, against bitter
sweet sunsets

16. the dis-

17. you know

18. you must know

19.

20. [left intentionally blank]

21. C-a thought

(more history   always his)
why he carried 50-pound bags of concrete for a nickel an hour
why he carried the world for a dime a day

why she carried babies and babies and babies

why she carried fence posts and bricks
why she carried babies and eggs and more
eggs than babies

baby why they fell
baby why they rose
baby why   they   baby

why he resented his mapped
face   dry rivers reaching around
eyes   flowing into drying/dying pools
why he resented the sunhot concreteness of the day
why he resented she
why she resented he
why she (re)s(c)ent
why
period
.

22. the silent sandwichmaker

23. the gambling machine
the gambling queen
the queen of clubs

24. the lucky

25. slot
slut
slit
[pick a vowel]

26. [try again]
slot

27. cha-ching

28. quick
quick

a show

29. click
click
bang

30. coonskin cap

31. snakeskin boots

32. lambskin vest

33. a John-Wayne hero/sonofabitch/pieceashit/sinner/lover of
[pick a word/phrase]
 working for a nickel a day laboring in concrete bags and dead   ends

34. uphill

35. through mud
and wind

36. the heat rising too fast   too far for the I to see

37. workin for a livin

38. to get a bitch

39. a business man in bibs and sweet sweat

40. an outlaw
with   out   law

41. the god of small things

42. C-amongst

the unknown
discarded
aborted
hidden

amongst miles of black
soil glinting of arrowheads
swallowing pottery/poetry whole
swallowing nature
a swallowing hole
miles of single blades singing through
the darkness
through the decades
of corn knee high
a jungle above big-headed dreams
con
sequence
reeking of reward
dreams laughing back
words

amongst baked waves as far as they could see, as far as

43. C-with

44. out

45. C-a silent film

46. C-with language
no and don't and no and stop and no and please and please and no

47. pleas

48. C-deleted

49. C-reaped

50. without language

51. the chop
ping of chickens' heads   watching them run   blind

52. Land-raped

53. a sick secret

54. a wish(bone) broken

55. a lady on the streets
a tramp

56. a starlet

57. waiting

58. to be discovered

59. waiting

60. for the drama

61. lunging for word/back word

62. Janus

63. begging

64. Let's play Pick a Vowel
slot
slit
slat

65. [try again]
slut

66. a winner
or not

67. C-a story

68. C-the daughter of lay-bore or labor

69. the daughter of sepia-toned bounty

70. hunter   s [space/time/space/time/space]

71. a lover of Little Joe and Marty Robins

72. Hum(p)bert's love child
Festus and Miss Kitty's best kept secret.

73. the disobedient pupil of Saints (and clauses).

74. a Dolly Parton wannabe

75. sweet

76. seXXX

77. Lolita

78. [time to process]

79. C standing in a field

80. that grows girls
each dressed in an almost dress/almost shirt
long hair flowing backwards
backlit faces
arms across chests
growing from the corn

stalkers
waiting to be p(r)icked

81. ripe, they say
for the plucking
[pick a consonant cluster]

82. big arms scoop her up

place her on a stand
she pretends to faint and rolls off
landing with her head in the silt
mulberry-stained feet in air

83. her best side up

84. big arms scoop her up
place her on a stand
she pretends to faint and rolls off
landing face first in the mud
ass in the air

85. her best side up

86. big arms scoop her up
place her in a box
strap her down
break her of falling

87. she misses the field

88. the wattery air

89. C-cloistered with a wolf, a lie, and an oiled bird

90. C-spinning free

91. the huffing and puffing

92. that cannot happen

93. C-a trace

94. an outlaw

95. of morality

96. faker [pick a vowel] of reality

97. a realization that her aging body is turning her basket of eggs into

little
mongoloid
children

98. if she doesn't
close the sex
fact or-y

99. according to her mother

100. C-a repetition, a name
CC Sahara with a dry smile
CC Symphony when she sings
CC Sadness when she cries
CC Shabang when she laughs
CC Shaboom when she's sex
CC Sailing
CC Sale

CC Sur(e)lynot

BABY C

X^0. C on a fencepost above a black and blue eggshell mosaic over dust and clover. A metallic light baby glowing over and over against sun.

X^1. C in white (   ), a plastic basket from Uncle Ed's Emporium and Mite Market, a one buck basket full of baby and flesh, full of stories and secrets in waiting, in need.

X^2. C a wad of flesh flashing through plastic weave, a crow resting on her shoulder, two kaleidoscope geese, standing on a mosaic, honking, flapping, tossing.

X^3. C surrounded by that color: basket, down, cloud, seeds, petals, skin, puff, and

X^4. C sings, notes misinterpreted. C sings, Take me home. And, Country roads. And, Sweet home. And, Where O where can this baby be.

X^5. C creating rules out of colors and symbols and sounds or statuses that wrap around her ear. Drums.

      A.   l w a y s

                        all   ways

      B.   a lady

                  a Good Girl

                  shhhhhhhhut your

      C.   Never

                  Never ever ever

                  under any circumstance

                  in any setting

                  regardless of

                  do Not

                  do naught(y)

X^6. C growing in a basket, her flash poking through the weave, skin tanning in square inches and acres and miles and millimeters of baby, geese at dawn, honking, Wake up, C. Honking, Ditch the plastic. Honking, Come out and play. Honking, Are you hungry. Honking, Eat crow.

Honking, Please, C. Please don't tease us.

Geese flapping at noon. Flapping, Hot. Flapping, How does this feel. Do ya like it. Do ya. Flapping, Come down and play. Flapping, You're good, C. You're a good, good girl. Flapping, Are you hot. Flapping, Come down and play in the wings, play in the breeze. C, Are you hot. C, Throw that crow out. Come on, C. Please, C.

Pleas.

Geese tossing down at dusk, C, are you chillin. Tossing smack, Boo. Don't cry, Baby C. Tossing, Catch this. Cover up. Tossing what falls back in their faces. C, Are you cold. Pluck that crow. Don't be afraid of the dark. Tossing, We can't see you. You're fading. C, Where are you.   C, What's with the crow.

X^7. There's a baby in a basket on a fence post down a country road, a crow on her head, geese beneath her post. She's flashing through the weave and nobody knows. Nobody cares. Nobody understands. The baby cries and sings.

Tractors roll on by on rocks. Trucks kick dirt into her basket. Cars buzz past, passengers catcalling. Geese ring. The crow releases a mess on the baby's head and caws.

I'm an orphan, cries the babe. I'm no lovechild. No love. No child. Rescue me, Sugar. Rescue me, Daddy. Rescue me.

X^8. A goose flaps, Mine. A goose flaps, Mine. A baby sings, Mine. Geese lock down on the necks of each other and begin to smack wings. Turbulence lifts a basket full of fleshy body.

Honk and slap and the breaking of feathers and wings or necks. The baby floats before falling into the theory of the road. Two geese lie. Flat. Circle a post. Eyes blink. Shut or wide. A baby basket in the gravel. The baby sings, Where O where can this baby be. And, A change is gonna come.

X^9. Baby C looking for Hot Momma or Sweet Daddy, crawls down the road, gravel harassing. Her knee cracks. A crow riding on her back, Baby C sings, Nobody knows. The crow caws. Sun blinks shut with baby sleeping amongst tiger lilies busy closing their wide yawns. Dawn rises. Tigers wake and open wide. C tickles their stamens.

A Motorcycle Momma trips by, scoops up the scored baby. They ride, crow flying high. Baby, drawing metaphors out of Motorcycle Momma's mouth, resting against her leather, being slapped by fringe, suffers loss and lost and love she does not understand. Baby feels the beat of the road, a feral incantation. C wiggles out of Motorcycle Momma's arms, hits the ground balling, slides into a culvert, crow falling from sky.

X^{10}. A basketless baby panting amongst cattails and bullfrogs and a spanking new patch of lilies, thinking about how she ditched Motorcycle Momma, struggling to remember what she left. Behind.

X^{11}. Crow caws, Mine. Baby sings, Mine and Why O why can this baby be. Crow blowing, makes a mess on scored baby's back. Cattails beat against windwaves. Lilies yawn wide, stamen flashing against tempos. Bullfrogs compose love songs on high, casting shadows beneath the scene.

X^{12}. Crow taunts, dirty baby. Nasty girl. Baby sings, What O what can this baby be. Crow fades into sky. A black circle closing in on itself. Empty basket. Lost. Baby sits on roadside bordered by wagging, singing, yawning.

CC N YOU

You wanted to touch the bow of her lip, thought it would feel like velvet or grass or silt.

You wanted to spank her, because it would be good for her, because it would teach her, because it would help her remember not to, because it would be good.

You wanted to kiss her eyes, because they were dark, because they spoke to you, because they blinked in codes you wanted to taste.

You wanted to touch the curve of her thumb, it looked strong. You liked the way it moved when she patted the cat, when she peeled potatoes, when she played guitar.

You wanted to push against her shoulders, because they were strong, angular, because you wanted to know how much she would give, wanted to see if she would break or fall, wanted to feel her f(r)ail.

You wanted to eat her breath, because you thought it would taste like cinnamon or blue or cumin.

When she passed you, she cut through air and time, avoiding

Her scent climbed rising heat, advancing up your body a little bit and more.

Her breath working around your space as if it didn't want you, but you thought

Her long hair wrapped loose around her neck, around her face, around her curve, reaching out toward you before falling away.

You called to her
called
to

her
she said

You offered wishes wrapped in tiny spells, rapped in tempo, measuring her
cunning, her pulse.

You offered to look away, didn't mean it.

You turned your face away from hers, tasted the air for her scent, imagined what
it was you could not see.

She was a delicate pain, growing on your spine. So subtle, she felt like tenderness,

like

Her voice traveled on invisible threads connecting your body to

Her eyes
Her teeth
Her fingers and hips

and the curve
haunted you, st(r)ained you.

You had to have these things
to touch them
without touching

with
out

As you moved toward her, your stomach bent inward, your eyed trembled, your
step skimmed the earth.

As you shifted

toward her

Her stationary, holding the wind, the sunrays, the second and minute, the days and centuries.

As you pushed toward her, she slipped away, just out of reach where you could
only perceive or miss.

You wanted to touch the bow of her lip, thought it would feel like thyme or
winter.

You wanted to eat her breath, thought it would taste like citrus or shadows
missed.

You called
    to her

                              she said

Baby Stories

Story1: A baby is born. It is born inside out, the heart flutters beyond its cage, intestines slithering past their walls, spiraling around the body, circling legs, suffocating stories. The little heart beats. The parents see the heart beat, cannot look at the face until the heart stops. The face is pink, then gray and blue. They bury the baby in a cedar box beneath an oak tree. Every day for 31 years, the mother swears she sees the baby's eye or toe or face in the sweet angles and curves of the tree's bark. Every day for 31 years, the father works. For a few years, he pretends not to think about the baby. After that, he believes he does not think about the baby. Every day for 31 years, the parents do not speak of the baby. Friends who ask are told it was a false pregnancy. There are no more babies because there is no more sex.

Story 2: There is a baby born and nobody wants her. She is, after all, a girl. She is carried to the side of the river and tossed away. She cries when her skin smacks against the cold, gray water, but the cries do not last. As she floats away, there are little fish searching for soft eyes and flesh. There are large fish tasting for baby. Once she hits the water, she feels nothing. They say, Babies aren't human until they are dressed. This baby never wore a dress.

Story 3: There is a baby born. In the beginning she belongs to one father or another and one mother. The first father tells the second father that he can keep the baby because the first father doesn't have enough time or money or breast milk to support the baby. Since the second father possesses the mother (and therefore the breast milk) and because he owns 400 acres of cropland, he should have the baby. So the second father takes the baby, not knowing who she truly belongs to. He calls her his.

Story 3: There is a baby born to a mother who doesn't really need a baby to keep her man. She places the baby in a plastic basket (because she cannot find her nicer wicker basket) and sets that basket on a fencepost on a dirt road. The mother selects that particular fence post because there are two good geese at the bottom to guard the baby, and because the road is isolated enough that nobody will see her dump the baby but not too remote, so somebody might find the baby with the intention of keeping it. There is also a creek, tall grass, and a lot of wild berries in the area, so the baby, when it learns to pick berries and eat grass, will have plenty to eat. A lot of individuals claim this baby.

Story 4: A babyless mother on a Harley sees a infant checkered with sunburn, covered in dust, sitting on a roadside in a patch of lilies and cattails. The babyless mother scoops up the baby and puts it on the Harley's gas tank. Together, the two ride until the babyless mother and the motherless baby are lulled into a state of near sleep by the good vibrations of the Harley. Eventually, the baby rolls off of the gas tank into a new patch of lilies. Oblivious to what is happening, the babyless mother remains babyless when she cannot remember whether or not she really had a baby for a few hundred miles or if it was the lack of sleep and her tendency to eat horseweeds that had her only thinking she had a real baby and was no longer babyless. For the rest of her life, the babyless mother sends silent prayers and incantations to the once-hers baby. The sounds of the babyless mother morph and grow as they reach the baby who is, eventually, no longer a baby.

Story 5: There really is no such thing as a baby.

Story 6: A father who loves his baby for reasons he cannot understand (because he has never met the baby but can only imagine what it is like to have a baby) can only imagine that the baby must love him back, because that is what babies do. This father thinks about his baby, the same baby that he gave to another man. As he thinks about this baby, new stories begin to form in his mind. He pictures himself washing the baby, feeding and watering it. He imagines dressing it for school, watching it ride away on the school bus wearing clothes he made from sheep and goat skins. He imagines the baby wearing a feed cap he found at the grain elevator. He imagines making fishing poles out of branches from an old oak tree and fishing for crappies and bluegills, filleting the fish, and having cookouts behind the house where he imagines the baby will grow strong from eating mutton and potatoes and fish and dirt. He imagines how tough the baby will be from wrestling hogs to the ground and chasing geese. He imagines the baby living with him forever, forever letting him hold and feed it.

Story 7: Ladies who find themselves pregnant out of wedlock should make sure the baby is either not born (by eating controlled amounts of rat poison or by drinking castor oil or by having somebody jump on the prospective mother's stomach or by use of a stick aimed at the problem) or go into hiding for a long enough period to have the baby to be discarded (in a river, feed to livestock, or abandoned in a wooded area) or left on the doorstep of a church very early on a Sunday morning.

Story 8: Possible fathers of babies produced out of wedlock should pay off the mother or enter into an undetermined period of emphatic denial. Of course, there is nothing to be ashamed of. As a man, one has certain needs that have to be fulfilled.

Story 9: A baby is born to a married mother and father. This, in itself, is nothing extraordinary. In fact, this is how babies are supposed to be born. This baby lives with the mother and father for nearly 9 long years doing baby things and getting the sort of attention babies crave, things like: food and water, clothing, a temperature controlled climate of approximately 60 degrees in the winter and 85 in the summer. The baby is held an average of 7.3 times a day through the age of 9 months, 6.77 times a day from 9 months to 17 months at which time the holding is decreased to 4.85 times a day for the baby's own good. By the time of the baby's third birthday, when there is a cake and a father wearing a clown wig, the frequency of being held graduates to 0.4 times per day. Being mature, the baby learns to do simple chores and is ready to be on its own for hours at a time by the age of 5.129, and, by the age of 8.56, the house smells too much of mature baby and the mother has to leave in search of herself, a self that is lost almost immediately after the birth of the baby, a self that is particularly slippery and illusive, for the mother has been searching for this self for most of her life (or at least since the age of 8.56). Shortly after, the father understands the depth of the baby's self-sufficiency and spends weeks at a time at meetings and conventions or working the fields or at the homes of special friends, the baby learns to make both toast and omelets, how to collect eggs and milk from the farm animals and berries and vegetables from the garden. Eventually, the baby, understanding how mature it really is, leaves the home in search of a job and a dog with which it can share leftovers.

Story 10: An abandoned baby is found in a trash barrel. The baby is abandoned by a 24-year-old mother who is later charged with attempted murder. Had she left the infant at a fire station, police department, or doctor's office (it is not clear whether this office has to be that of a medical doctor) there would have been no charges filed. Five years prior to this incident a baby is found under a stairwell and later adopted. The same year a 15-year-old can't tolerate the shame or grief or depression that sometimes accompanies the birth of a baby out of wedlock or the birth of a baby to a teenager, a teenager who might be called a whore or a slut or a bitch or a worthless piece of shit that should have been aborted herself or murdered or taught a lesson through rape or another form of physical pedagogy. A year later (and having learned a lesson about how abandon babies might be discovered), a 16-year-old places her newborn in a garbage bag before dropping it in a shed behind her house. This baby is not adopted. Two years before a baby is abandoned in a trash barrel by a 24-year-old mother somewhere in the south, a baby is found alive under a tree at a hospital. Since there must be a doctor's office in the vicinity, it is likely that the mother, if found, will be able to declare amnesty.

Story 11: An 18-year-old man is charged with raping a 5-month-old baby girl while her mother is in class at the local high school. The baby (who requires surgery and cries hard enough to either vomit or overfill her lungs with melancholy) might have been crying too loud for the man to tolerate or the man might have been on drugs or drunk or the baby might have been asking for it or the man might have just needed to satisfy a primal urge to dominate or to get off. Fifty years earlier, a mother castrates her newborn son. The infant's screaming or the shame of having a disfigured child or the understanding of the possible spiritual or legal consequences is too much, it works its way into the mother, slips through her cells as she lines up a revolver to the temple of the infant's head, then to her own. She pulls the trigger once. A century earlier a father rapes a 10-month-old daughter who bleeds to death and is placed (along with several rocks and flowers) in a burlap sack and sent to the bottom of a river that flows into the Mississippi and then into the Gulf of Mexico. It is unclear how far the body, bricks, burlap, or flowers travel before being consumed by fish or mud.

Story 12: A baby is born dead, the cord wrapped around the neck. Two days earlier, the mother complains of a series of violent movements in her womb and calls her doctor who says that there is absolutely nothing to worry about and to stop overreacting and that he will see her at her next appointment and that the baby will be still for a few hours to a day before it is born, which it is. The baby is still, and it is born.

I

I
daughter
lover
depository
refuse
to claim
victim
or dead
or sorrow

II
abandon
pushing against
earth
and desire
digesting
rage   churning it
into rage or
sex
u
al
I
ty

III
girl
woman
daughter
not

IIII
dirty
girl

IIIII
dirty

IIIIII
broken
dis   carded
thick
headed or thighed

IIIIIII
re
claimed
daughter of de
sire
lover of r
age
or
dream   ons
or

IIIIIII
all about
The
Body

IIIIIIII
all about the
curve
and
gaping   mouth

IIIIIIIII
a   bout
(of)
desire

IIIIIIIIII
sex be
coming
fiction
becoming
poetry
or nothing
trickling down
into a fun(nel)
of sweet

IIIIIIIIIII
rage

BOYFRIENDS

First boyfriend looks like Barry Manilow. I introduce myself as Mandy Lola Lolita. He says he's no Manilow, but I keep him around, wait for him to sing. Nothing. Every Sunday he takes me to the roller rink. Actually Sugar Daddy takes me and he rides his bicycle. We have a sortadate date. He can roller skate. I can spin and play Pacman. He watches. That's it. He says nothing. He doesn't sing, but I hold his hand and root beer for weeks, because I am waiting for a song. Waiting to taste his whitebrown hair.

Second boyfriend looks like David Bowie. I hold his arm. Call him Ziggy. He looks sideways. At me. He isn't quite angular enough, so I feed him grass and corncobs. I make him chase me, but, still, his jaw line isn't quite Bowie. I can't make out those solid blue lines beneath his pastel surface. He doesn't sparkle. He won't dance. Refuses to move me.

Third boyfriend smells like Richard Dawson from his *Match Game* days. I sink into his hair and breathe. He touches my face, rests his mouth on my hand. He smells like aftershave and forest, like ginger and diluted Polo, like matches burning out. The carnation on his lapel is silk. Petals saturated with dust mites. Tiny little pests draw a line between a match and love. He calls me Darling and Honey and Sugar and Babe. I stop him before Babe becomes Baby. He is smooth on the hands. When I speak into his microphone, he vanishes.

Fourth boyfriend acts like Luke Duke, but I like Bo. I chase Bo on my motorcycle but can't hook him. Luke chases me around on a school bus, crying, Daisy. His lips pushed out away from the disappointed stubble on his face. He tracks me until I reach an edge he cannot cross due to probation or because he runs out of fuel. Bo, I say, chasing on my pony. Come, I say. Back, I say.

Fifth boyfriend is Steve Martin. Maybe he is married or old or otherwise unavailable. I ask him how he got so funky. So funny. He says he's not even trying. He has white hair and an expensive smile—teeth lined up like silver bars in a crate. His skin is matte and clear. His hands too soft. I wait for his routine. Wait for a joke, but he just looks at me. I try but cannot laugh. He is not wild. I am not crazy.

Next boyfriend walks like Scott Hamilton. I buy ice skates and take him to the pond. Skate, I say. Can't, he says. I lace up the skates and show him how to go backwards and spin. I don't know how to go forward. I can do a back flip, I say. I can't, he says. What a waste of a good walk. The gloss on his forehead fails in the sun. The shine cannot spark against the clear, sweet snow. Do anything, I say. He says something. I say, What. He says, Nevermind. Never mine.

Seventh boyfriend looks like Mikhail Baryshnikov. He doesn't dance. I say, Just stand there. He does. I hold his hand, kiss his forehead, show him to my friends. I say, Do something foreign. He puts his arm around me and says things that ring Russian. I say, Okay. He releases more language, things that sound like a battle or history. This is Russian for love. Or, Give me a drink. Or, Kiss my neck. I do all three. He winks. We start over.

Eighth boyfriend does not look or smell like Little Joe. He is neither Pa, nor heaven. He is not that kind. His teeth lie crooked in his mouth. My fingers walk through his curls until he stops breathing. He vanishes into a young Mac Davis, is less manageable, sings in jokes. I slip into his mouth looking for magic. There is none. The spunch line is buried beneath his tongue. I can't move it. It is too heavy. It is anchored by a hemp frenulum—the knot tightens every time I touch him.

Next boyfriend is Marty Robins. He wears a cowboy hat and calls me Senorita. The roses on his shirt smell like mothballs and dust, like needlework and sundown. His gun shines like his teeth. He plays his guitar. Says, I love you, CC. He says, One little kiss. I try, but the thorns on his appliqué slice my skin, separating it into a second mouth. He licks his lips, reaches for my new, bloody opening. I shoot, Good-bye. There is no white stallion. No setting sun.

Tenth boyfriend is painted like Adam Ant. I dress like Madonna and we go to a club. We drive and drink a six-pack. We dance. We weave through light rays, strobes tapping against hours and paint or shapes and sighs. Sex hangs on guitar riffs, bounces off techno beats, refuses to go home at closing time. He moves in and out of my space, making sure the crowd gets his good side—his good side. I slip in front of him, flashing my own better side to a mob of bigheaded performers. Unappreciated, we abandon the tempo. Slip into the vanishing wave of manufactured rhythm.

Last boyfriend is Beverly Hills Eddie Murphy. He has a sporty, rusted car. He moves fast. I talk. He produces that laugh. I want to take him home and keep him but cannot remember where home is. Or if there ever was a home. He asks if I party all the time. I say, Never. Hardly ever, I mean. I reach for him, but he's rolling away. Stop, I say. Stop. His ride roars, shoving my voice aside. He is heading toward Malibu Mansion or Somewhere Exotic, a space I cannot imagine, cannot read. Come back, I say. The road rock dust rolls in on itself. There are too many clouds to know whether the sun is setting or rising. I reach for his happy, black expression, moving to the reverberation of his laugh. When I reach it, he is not there.

CC Sleepless

A shadow flick- errs on CC's soul or curtain or in her closet. It is round and faint or bold and booming. CC and the shadow do not dance. She does not acknowledge the way it pushes against her she cracks eggs   draws conclusions and imag(in)es.

Be good, CC, the shadow hints. Be a good listener. You have it made, CC. Life is easy for a girl. Easy for a girl like you. Easy for you.   Easy. Do you hear. Do you   understand. CC sleeps,   every minute a disregard of the shadow. She does not listen, snaps a pillow over her earholes, wiggles her legs in hopes of exhaustion or the appearance of violence in her habit. She closes her eyes, a do not disturb sign on her   body.

Don't deny where it is you come from, CC, the shadow means to say. It is hard for me, the shadow does not say.

Every time CC wakes, she feels
that shadow on her
ceiling, maw gaping wide, shades of liquid,
dripping   down,
reaching toward her and pulling or spreading
inside her and pushing or just
                              searching.

Fall

              in

                              g

              away when she lunges toward
the shadow that fades into
the creases of   CC's   structure.

Give in, CC. Relax. Easy, CC. Be still. Hush.
(Re)member.

Hoping it is a dream or illness or a
coincidence with habit, CC moves her bed

into another room. She pulls the black shades, crushes

traces of light trying to get closer to

In the darkness, the shadow reverses itself to paler shades of discomfort. It soft(ly) chants in (re)imagined tones of discontent.

Just when CC understands what it wants, the shadow changes form and tone.

Keeping still as CC's leg begins to shake, the shadow fades into the darkness where it waits and (re)forms.

Leave me alone, CC chants. Just leave.
Me alone.
Not Yours.

    Casting, shadow (re)moves.

Out.

Please, CC. Listen. Understand. Life is easy for a girl. Easy for a girl like you.

Quit.
Realize, CC. You are soul/sole, past/passed, hope.   Stop.

This is love.
Un(Moved) to tear(s).

Varying declarations.
Wake up, CC. Do you know… CC.
          Do you   remember…
                 Do
                      yo…?

SeXXX, the voice does not say, slapping
sheets.   Slapping…   Stop, she says.
And, (k)no(w).

You (mis)understand. This is a story, (re)
action, collaboration, our
art, my story, your
piece/peace.

                         Yours

Ours

To get you to your   to get us to our   to
reach   beyond   to reach   to make it to
(y)our   own to your own to
                    your end to your

own   end.
Zinnas growning in desire
         above

                    your

              at   your

                    at   the

                              end   .

CC Rider

CC in a Pinto, driving into dusk, in dust, evergreens reaching into the wake, slapping what is behind away. CC driving toward time in reverse, toward obsession.

CC in fifth, weaving her way through a web of unknown gravel or mud or grass covered paths, driving a Pinto without tags, without gauges, without directions.

CC parking in fields behind brambles and brush to sleep, to sweat, pees in the woods on the trees, wets ant hills or a bumper.

CC thinking of figures she cannot picture, tigers and bares, thinking of tails and lilies.

CC searching mindbanks, riding on waves of difference and mysterious nostalgia, thinking about motorcycles. Remembering what she cannot imagine.

CC starving, stops by a cornfield tasseling in the sun, heat waving above the blacktop. CC parking the Pinto, rips off ear after ear after ear, tearing away shuck and silk, chews her way across the cob, hits return, chews some more.

CC with eighty bucks and a dress in a burlap bag. Pinto needs fuel. CC with less money, less drive, (re)vision in motion.

CC works her way cross counties, cross-country. Go west, young CC, says the road. Motorcycle Momma hurls textboxes floating on wind swells. A call for CC, for Baby C.

CC at a dead end feels flashes behind her.

CC panics. CC panics. CC panics.

CC reasons with herself. Forward toward the calls or backward toward the flashes.

CC turns Pinto left. It can only turn left and left and left to go back. Did she only imagine those bursts. In 800 feet, she turns left again and left.

CC drives forward, thirty dollars to go. She's hungry. She sees (w)rappers on the road and knows there is no place in them for her story. She drives, hits a bump and Delilah comes on the radio. What would you say to her, asks Delilah. A voice whispers, I know. Delilah says, Just tell her. Voice says, I am. Delilah surrenders, Every breath you take...Honey...Darling.

CC turns left into abandoned barn. Sleeps cold. Dreams about Sting, tigers, and plastic baskets. Sting chases her. He carries a plastic basket full of baby tiger. Sting's lips are moving, but the tiger purrs too loud. CC only sees lips shift. Sting trips over rock. Baby tiger rolls out of basket, fur scored, still purring. Tiger tracks CC. A bat cracks Pinto's window awake. CC's dream falters. Dies. She is thinking about Beverly Hills and his smile. She wonders if a smile can be that bright, if it is real or plastic, if the laugh is live or Memorex.

CC turns the key, goes backwards toward the flash, running over horseweeds, soybeans, and aluminum cans before spinning back and forward. Pinto rocks and runs. Singing, CC rides toward sun rising, toward incantations of scotched breath or life or away from the flashing/fleshing.

DREAM

RUNNING LOVE

Running Love bathing dirty girl, clearing debris from hair, untangling locks, rubbing oil on burnt skin, on pale skin, moving back and forth in rocker, sings Aa-amaz-ing Grace…how sweet the babe

Running Love feeding baby berries and peas, rolling dough, making gravy, roasting beef and beast

Running Love filling baby with warnings about wolves and cougars, about boys and money, and girls, about voices and (mis)perceptions

Running Love hemming skirts up and down at a baby's will, patching holes in denim that baby made with sandpaper and scissors, darning socks and dogs

Running Love tapping baby's back, baby crying about names she's called

Running Love telling a baby tales of spirits and wanderers, tales of talking pigs and princesses who didn't need princes

Running Love blowing on baby's scrapes, spraying peroxide and Bactine

Running Love churning ice cream for yearly celebrations of baby's approximate day of birth

Running Love singing crying baby to sleep, shaping the Beatles, Johnny Cash, Marty Robins, Loretta Lynn, Elvis, The Monkees

Running love running when baby screams at a spider or mouse, at a voice or shadow

Running Love adding and multiplying or subtracting and dividing numbers in baby's books, sprouting rhymes and songs to help baby remember equations and histories she least wants to know

Running Love holding baby close, letting

baby

g o

DELIVERANCE

Momma measures C. This won't work, she says. The 38 is good, but the 39 is too much. The big 31 in between needs to come down at least four or five. You know the formula, she says pinching C's waist.

C pulls away. Stop it, she cries. I don't care. Go away.

Momma says, This is for your own good. You know. To get a man. A good man. One with means.

Which means what, asks C.

With means, I said. Momma spins. Sugar Daddy likes it like this. She laughs.

Gross, sings C.

That's not what Daddy says. She grabs at her own waist. There isn't an inch here to pinch.

Leave Me A Lone.

Seriously, C. Do you want a man or not.

I want a dog.

You'll end up with a dog, a poor bastard like Sweet Daddy, an old crow, a ditch weed, a frog flat broke on the road.

C walks, Good. I like crows and frogs.

And do something with that hair. It makes you look poor. A good man won't want a project. Men don't want rags. They want dolls. Be a doll.

A goooood man would be a project. She pulls her bangs back tight, stretching her eyebrows into disbelief. I'll shave this head. How's that.

Be serious, C. Gentlemen prefer blondes, Momma says, mad, flipping her hair. Momma tries to run her fingers through C's hair. Why is it always like a horse tail, like brambles thick with rodents.

It is called bed head. I've been in bed with shady characters.

Don't say that. Momma raises her hand. People will think you're a tramp.

C moves away. Leave this tramp alone.

I love you, Baby C. Don't talk like that.

C sings, C and all the people sittin in a tree F U C—

Momma's knuckles thrust against C's cheekbone, a ruby slices open skin beneath eye, the memory of a diamond etched in her dimple.

C smacks back. I'm outta here.

Momma gathers the loose material of C's shirt and reels.

Have some respect, she spits in C's face.

C swings.

You missed. Momma lets loose of the gather, pushes C to the floor.

Go to your room.

C lies on her back.

I said, Go to your room.

Which one.

Your bedroom.

The one I sleep in or the one I puh-lay in.

Go to your room.

C is still.

Get up.

You put me here. You get me up.

Get up.

C is silent.

Get up.

You put me here.

Momma kicks at C's legs. Move.

C is stiff.

Momma kicks again. Get out of here.

C sings, Mommaaaaaaaa. Ooooouuuu.

Stop it.

No escape from realiteeeeeeeeeeeeeeeeeeeeeeeeeee.

Momma kicks C's thigh.

Life had just begun.

Get out of here.

Nothing really matters

Get.

toooooo meeeeeeee.

Momma points to the door.

tooo-oo meeeeee. C gets up.

Now leave.

You can't throw your little darlin out, cries C. Help me, Sugar Daddy, she cries. Rescue me, Sweet Daddy. Why is everybody always pickin on me.

Momma recoils. Strikes.

C is still.

Stop bleeding tears.

C is silent.

Now go.

C sings, I am going. I won't be back.

You'll be back. You like Sugar Daddy's bucks as much as I do.

C spits. Walks away.

Come back, Baby C. I didn't mean it. I love you.

She turns, You're mad.

I'll call the cops. I'll tell them you're a runaway.

Go ahead. I'll tell them you're a monster. I'll show them these scars, she says, placing her hand over her heart. She grabs her crotch and sings, whoooooooo-oo. She walks a moon. Uses sign language to signal her departure.

Please, C. You're all I've got.

I am not yours.

You are mine.

Good-bye.

You can't go. You're not old enough. For God's sake.

I am in dog years.

Come back, she pleas. She sobs.

Any

    way

        the wind

VOICES

10% of her life gone, she sits awake with a new cassette recorder trying to capture the voices, hoping to gather proof of their existence, yearning to be understood.

Voices wrap around her mind, puncture perception. Voices call to her when she sleeps, they travel through her veins, speaks in tiny phrases. Voices chanting history, her story, tales she accepts as hers swimming just beyond the tip of her reach. She tastes the grit of the earth on each word, the sweet and sweat of hide and marrow. She tastes the dark powder, the sulfur, the tinge of time, circling her buds, engraining little receptors with hints of (miss)story.

20% of her life gone, she tries to ignore the incantations, certain what she evades will vanish. She attempts to void the unavoidable.

Voices snake through her gray matter as she washes a dish or peals a potato. Voices move into the most sacred of mindspaces where they reside, growing in number and strength, becoming, before she understands what is happening, part of her own vocabulary, part of her existence, part of her dictionary of truth.

30% of her life gone, she begins transcribing their tinny articulations into a leather journal. Eventually the journal is swallowed by her desire to become something she is not, some thing she can never be.

Voices dancing above flames in the blue and yellow heat of that which sets her kind apart from others, those so much a part of her past/present that she cannot draw a clear line in the silt, cannot (un)imagine what it is she (mis)perceives. Her (re)readings tainted by stories that come in phrases and clauses, come disguised as vocabulary or history or little moral lessons of being (whatever it is she will become).

40% of her life gone, she sketches sounds that ring through her peripheral. Echoes morph into imagery and artistry rather than the concrete evidence she hoped to create.

Voices of grand pasts decorated in the sort of nostalgia that makes murder or rape or robbery shine like ice against evergreen backdrops lit by sharp rays of sun slipping past the gate kept by black ink on yellowing cotton, slipping past little tainted tales. Voices of futures so big and hot that they can only fail at (re)creation, at coloring, at (re)placing reverberations, can only (mis)imagine the curve of a girl or the scent of a life lived beneath heavy shadows of melancholy idea(l)s.

50% of her life gone, she attempts to engage the sounds in conversation. The talks are multi dimensional—her talking to them, them speaking to her, her pleading, them taunting/haunting, her weeping, them pushing down on her body, her voice, her soul.

Voices in surround sound. High (in)fidelity. Volume graduating from merely anticipated to the boom of thunderheads intimidating atmosphere and earth, chanting, (dis)closure. Voices spear her reality, pausing to take (snap)shots of her confidence, stopping to press against her will(ingness) to (be)come ((back) story).

60% of her life gone.

Rap. (W)rapping.

70% of her life gone, she absorbs the voices, is studied, is locked away with crazy people. She cannot believe.

Voices give her directions, demand her attention, push her to glimpse what she cannot grasp, calling her to the west to the south and north, begging her to move. Away.

80% of her life gone and she joins the voices in a marriage. Til death do them part. For better or worse. For better. For Worse. For the best. For the worst. For.

Voices wrap around her mind, puncture consciousness. Voices call to her when she sleeps, travel through her veins, speak in tiny phrases that she absorbs, (re)writes, overtakes, overturn. Overjoy. Over.

She ends up miscalculated. Tries to quantify misses and takes. Confuses the flow of time. Buries her figure.

Her life gone.
Her living.
Her living her life.

Gone.

RELATIONS

She is standing in a ditch, lilies licking her legs. She is a toddler,
is twenty or twelve. She is an infant or retiring.

Motorcycle Momma rides a dust wave, stops in front of her.

C notices the face for the first time, features soft. This is
Beautiful
Mother.

Mother's mouth moves.

C hears hums and strokes the soft breath of a melody, but there
are no words. She leans in closer to hear Mother's voice.

Mother opens her mouth wide, ready to swallow time or missed
understandings or the soul of an infant lost or found rolling on a
rocky road.

C slants in more. She cries, Shivers down my spine.

Mother pulls away. Her mouth says, Not now. Her voice roars,
dim and distant, meanings tangled in e-motion, snagged by
stalks of thyme.

C reaches out, grabs. An apparition of Beautiful Mother slips
through her palms, running down the river of a lifeline before
vanishing.

She is standing in a ditch, frogs composing a scene. She is a
thirty, is ten or a toddler. She is an infant.

Motorcycle Momma rides the wind, crashes in front of her.

C notices her hands for the first time, cracked and folded. These are the hands of Sweet Daddy, hands that move toward her face.

C's memories travel the valleys that line each knuckle, recovering flaming marshmallows on a stick, remembering rides on the fender of a rusted red tractor.

The second finger cut off mid-nail, points to something she cannot clarify, something mechanically ominous. It hovers in the air before bending away.

C sings, Put your hand in the hand. She turns her palm upward.

The hands touch and recoil.

An invisible knife tracing a vein from wrist to fingertip, C begs, Please don't. Go.

She is standing in a ditch, cattails scratching her inhibitions. She is ten, is twenty and a teen. She is old enough.

Motorcycle Momma waves, stops behind her.

C is still. She cannot turn around, is afraid to see. The voice sweeps through her hair. It belongs to Sugar Daddy.

The sound of vowels penetrate h-air.

She shakes.

Consonants click her thoughts into a-motion.

Stop, she says. And, I am not.

Language is born between clicks and vowels.

Too heavy, she says.

Phrases plot against space.

What are we doing here, she says.

It is the tongue of love.

What are we doing, she says.

It is the dialect of a daddy.

What are we, she says.

Prosets. Factions caught in thyme.

What are, she says.

Xxxpression.

What, she says.

Nothing.

She is bathing in a ditch, bee balm in her hair, snakes hissing
past. She is a child, an old woman, a downy bundle of tie-dyed
skin being born.

Motorcycle Momma arrives, thyme in her hair, rose on her hips.

C falls into her, the scent of lilac, of sage and orange, of
Running Love and history, rolling deep into her senses.

Love runs through but does not stop.

C feels heat and cold collide, congealing in her veins. It is a soft
pain. A lost pain. She un-covers.

Love wraps, raps, tangles, pushes. It brands her. Recollection
sitting soft against repression or depression or regression or
dangling on the sharp edge of obsession.

C bows into pressure. She cries, Where or where has this Love gone.

Love runs. A-way. Slaps C a-wake. The underside of a pillow or sun-dried cotton sheet thick with grass and dandelion at-tempts. Desire descends. Through earth and time, toward the spine of an old tale. Running Love holding on, watering the flowers in C's hair.

C waiting to re-move the arms that bind or bend. Or mend.

She is standing in a ditch, lilies licking her lips. She is a toddler, is twenty or twelve. She is mo(u)rning.

Motorcycle Momma rides a lust wave.

C notices her face, this Beautiful Mother.

Mouth moves.

Hums and strokes soft breath.

Melody. No. Words.

Her mouth wide. Ready.

Soul of an infant lost and found rolling on rocks.

Shivers down the pine.

Meanings tangled in emotional notions.

Stalks of thighs.

Stalks

an apparition.

Beautiful
words
running
down
a river.

V
a
n
i
sh
i
n
g
.

ssshhhhhhh…

This is Beautiful Mother.

This is C.

Standing

or

falling

or

rolling.

CROW

Three pet roosters, blue-black tails, red backs and necks glow metallic in the sun as I dig. They jump in and out of the hole, searching for food.

When I find white grubs curled, waiting for next June or May, I scoop them onto the end of the shovel and feed the roosters.

I dig and tell them, This hole is not for you.

I dig through the yellow-black earth, past the roots of an elm, through tunnels of worms, because Cat has status, because he sat curled around my neck while the voices wrote and rewrote this story, because he sang and I listened, because he wrapped around my head and purred me to sleep when I thought I might die, because he couldn't resist following the voices, because voices lack teeth and tongue, because voiced don't bite, because sometimes a cat might chase a voice or maybe, just once, a cat called Cat might follow, may go too far.

I dig, not because this day is atypical. Although, a typical day might include voice and death.

This morning, the same dogs that sunned every day with Cat were eating his body. The dogs were sent away, their bellies brushing the ground in shame, shame because they couldn't resist the fresh meat, shame because they, while they were eating, were looking around between bone crunching bites to see if anyone, any human, was watching, shame because they knew if they didn't eat fast enough it would come to the yelling, to the damnits, to the rock throwing, to temporary banishment into the horseweeds, because the dogs, too, wondered how not to listen to voices.

My superstitions keep Cat waiting for the earth to swallow him almost whole, waiting to gradually be digested by time.

What will I do while the voices write now. There is no Cat. No Sugar or Sweet or Hot. There is no Momma. Neither Love nor Running.

Sweet Daddy taught me not to cry. He also told me these things: You are strong. This is how you hit without breaking your thumb. Don't hit like a girl. Make a fist. Step into it. Only hit if you have to. You cannot act like a girl. You are strong. Do not lie. I hate liars.

Sugar Daddy was more into showing me things. Making me feel when I did not want to feel. Any thing.

Running Love told me, God cleans house in the fall. Or was it the spring.

She meant that was when most people die. She died in early winter or maybe it was late fall. In the white bed fenced in stainless steel, I kissed her cold, gray forehead and touched her hand. The hand was like a fish, the head like a chilled ham in a dry skin. Old enough, I cried.

Sweet Daddy said, It's okay.

I think he meant to cry, but I don't know.

I realize I'm not digging. I'm standing beside a

big muddy hole full of roosters.

Get out, I say, poking them with the shovel.

Cat died from that thing they say most often kills cats. A vet would say a thing like, Worms. Or, Distemper. Or, Tire trauma. Or, Stupidity. Or, maybe, just once, Insanity. But I cannot pay to find out what I already believe. I can read the signs, can hear the tale forming out of repurposed consonants and vowels. Can feel the weight of their certainty.

I count the s(t/c)ars.

First is a chickenpox mark. I don't remember the pox or scratching   or anything.

I have a scar to remind me of what I can't remember.

Hot Momma said the pox scars are for disobeying the Do Not Scratch laws for children with pox or bug bites.

The second scar is from a horse wreck. I might have been seven. I might have been eight or six or smarter, but wasn't.

I dropped the reigns and rode up a hill, branches clawing at my face and arms. With both hands on the saddlehorn, I forgot to breathe, tried to reach the flapping strap.

Sweet Daddy jumped over the fence and took the reins. He offered me to Running Love and clutched the leather tethers with one hand, searching for a rock with the other. Palming the stone, he jerked the horse's head to eyelevel as he bashed the granite against the animal's head, over and over. Running

Love's voice ringing through ears, shrill and soaring. Sweet Daddy brought the horse down, panting. Sweet Daddy panting, covered in blood or shame. A horse wrapped in terror.

Sweet Daddy's face filled with hot life, his color so dark his features disappeared under the haze.

Running Love's voice washed over, accusing and forgiving. Sentencing.

What a pair, Sweet Daddy and C, bathed in blood and shame.

The longest scar is from Sugar Daddy's motorcycle, from giving Hot Momma a ride, from riding with my mother, the actress, from riding Sugar Daddy's bike in the mud, from having a rider out of balance from moving fast, faster than death; there was slick and tires and that rider chanting words like No and Stop and Slow and Down. The actress tried to jump, pushing the bike into Sugar Daddy's new machine shed, breaking his bike or trust. Waking his madness.

Hot Momma stubbed a toe, called the driver an asshole, and limped to the house, hand on forehead, crying.

Bitch, I called to her back. Whimp, I said. You are a baby—these words rode the ground beneath Hot Momma's mantra of sorrow.

Hip to thigh to calf, my jeans and skin were torn. I hid the wreckage, buried the jeans.

Damn it, I said pouring rubbing alcohol onto

the cut, Hot Momma sitting cross-armed, her complexion and mascara withering. She fumbled for pills. Reached out for remedies.

You can't hide that, she said, slapping my thigh. It'll scar, she said, smiling. Sugar Daddy doesn't like scars. On bikes. Or girls.

Anchoring the skin together with duct tape, I said nothing.

I dig a hole for the cat in the garbage sack who is waiting to be buried. The roosters continue to circle speaking chicken language.

I am a map drawn by my ancestors on foreign white skin, their query for privilege. I am a trinket, a treasure hunt written in crocked, puckered lines, directions for snipe hunting.

I stand in the rain, a hole at my feet with most of a cat in a garbage sack resting in soil. I push the heavy clumps of dirt onto the cat in the bag. Begging for grubs, hungry roosters scratch and chatter in nervous anticipation.

There aren't anymore, I tell them.

Please, they mean to say.

Be quiet, I say. This is a funeral.

Pray or something, I tell the roosters.

They keep scratching at the dirt.

Idiots, I say to them. Have some respect.

They realize they are all roosters and one chases another, chasing the third; they run off with wings spread wide, chests inflated, feathers ruffled, crowing chicken obscenities at each other, warning but not brawling, each letting the others know he's the rooster with the most status, asking if he's the rooster with the most status, none of them serious, none of them stopping to realize the hens are locked safely away in a pen solid against the penetration of predator or rooster and they are free to search for grubs, free to create war or peace.

CC SHABOOM

CC Shaboom, the virgin slut

CC tryin   lookin   looking

CC with a fro, with a Princess Layya, with the pigtails low, ponytail high, with lemon juice and peroxide, with Clairol

CC to dye, to die, with a Di

CC do-ya-wanna   hava a tongue in your ear

a hand down your   down the   down the

CC you-wanna, you-know-you-wanna,   Want It

CC do-ya-know

CC do-ya-wanna   have a tongue in   have a c— in

NO   No   no   n   o

CC by a candle or camp fire or burning building, by the hand inching in   the c— crowing   the c— crying

CC do-ya-wanna

CC with nipples the size of quarters, dollars, tuna cans

CC happy as an eraser, as a pin, as a pen, or was that w/horror

Hot Momma ~~M. D.~~

Slouching on a bench, Hot Momma drinks green tea. Says it is better than black or orange or maybe not. Hot Momma chants, Straight up—no sugar. Straight up, unleaded—as they say, whoever they may be.

Rocks. Rocks. Baby, bring me rocks.

Momma takes three Naproxen Sodium pills, a few Acetometephen (prescription-strength plus) and a children's aspirin. She pops a pair of allergy pills offering 24-hour relief and the letter D for Drug or Sudaphed, meaning the pharmacist has her driver's license number, her address, birth date, signature, and humility. She sees a different pharmacist every week for a box, takes Sundays off. She chants, Don't look at me. Stop. Look at me. Like what you see. Sugar. Love me. Pleas.

She monitors phone calls, dips behind the wooden part of the door, crouching (hidden), peeking up through the glass when someone knocks. Baby, tell them I was hit by a car. Tell them I moved out of the country. Tell them I'm gone. I am gone.

Maybe when they find me, she says, I'll be dead beneath a heap of broken glass and wood, trampled by a SWAT team holding a battering ram. She sings things like, Who can it be now? And, They've come to take me away? And, Why do they follow me?

She rubs pain relief cream on her temples, across her forehead, on her neck and chest. The menthol makes her shiver. She chants, Hot. Hot. Hot. It burns, Baby. It burns. She rubs capsaicin pepper on her shoulders, arms, and legs, reaching up and over and under and around to cover most of her back.

Momma sings, I am woman hear me roar. She growls.

She slips iron, calcium, B-complex vitamins, herbs. Edit yourself, she says. Edit. Edit. Work it out. Girl. Work it. Sugar. Love me. Please.

I have an infection she says, a wrist on her forehead. Feel it, Baby. Is it hot, she asks. Fetch me the Durapen. The syringe, too. In her thigh, she takes a dose for a 150-pound calf. The needle catches the skin as she pulls it away. Better, she says. Better. A little over for a body like this. A hot mother. Right. Sugar. Love.

She sits at her desk and starts her morning with internet weather, email, and tea. Baby gets dressed, finishes homework, kisses the cat, tosses the hamster a kernel of kibble, floats the fish a flake, hopes tenderness or drugs will kick in.

Momma asks, Should I toast a toast or scramble an egg. Three out of four doctors recommend breakfast for their patients who eat. Those who don't look damn good in a gown, cries Momma.

Baby smiles. A little. Looks at the cat.

Momma says, I am no crack addict—there is no anhydrous or drain cleaner in these veins—just blood, caffeine, and some little necessities. Good goods, Baby. Why do I always feel like somebody's watching me. Stop. Stop looking at me. Love me. Don't judge me. Stop. Looking at me.

Baby walks.   away

Momma stumbles to stove, holds the needle tip in the burner's flame as the scrambled eggs snap and pop into a state of dryness. The richardsimmons toaster throws black bread onto the floor in a fit of hyperenthusiasm. As the needle cools, she draws up 2 more ccs of Durapen (enough for a 200-pound calf). She flicks the syringe to release air bubbles. Penicillin, no gateway drug, sings Momma.

Stabbing the needle through her thigh, she calls Baby back to breakfast. Hot Momma turns on a heel, falls to the floor, places a wrist over her eyes.

Baby watches. Stares. Says, Should I call Sugar Daddy. Should I call 911. Search and Rescue. Should I call.

Momma says, No. And, Go to school. And, This pepper cream is starting to burn. Love me. Please. Love me, Tender.

C CHASES LOVE

Yellow hearts of icebergs bite her tongue as she swims through space toward the illusion, a destination in waiting, hunkered down, ready. She cannot see past walls of willows and elms forcing their way through history, through clay and fat atmosphere toward the hot of blue.

When she believes she finds love it looks like song, the rise and fall of a waltz floating on gravel, a tempo or tune growing out of blonde air, falling into ditch. This love cannot sing, refuses to vibrate into life. The butter does not fly. Words turn into worlds rolling into whitespace. Stories wait to be written by glossy, glassy voices.

C chases love   not knowing

The beat of a resistance stares back. She cannot be live, cannot feel the pulse of it. Letters circle round, lining up on lines, a terrible cliff standing guard over flags surrendering. She reaches out, touches this love, her hand sliding down curves too sharp to flavor too dull to shine. Desperately seeking a rhythm that will not pound, she moves this love that transcends writing on the road.

This love disappears into the small V of a crayon-crafted road draped on a MMMM-mountain range.

C chases

Love wearing a moustache and a red carnation presses lips against hand, winks in codes that say, O. And, Baby. And, O baby. Love wearing pale, thin lips over square, white teeth biting on tongue, biting on sorrow, biting on the flavor of bitter sweat.

She responds to love's call, pushes back against the old cliché of summers and winters that meet in the proper proportions of gender and sex(uality) and bea(t)uty, of her divided by him, provided by him, for him. The carnation fumes, too much for her delicate senses or for her arrogance—strange creature that she is.

C chases love, not knowing why

Impatient, love chases back—just once. Haunting the emptiness of a page, the story goes. Love speaks. Sound grows. Vowels swell. She cannot see past the hyperbole.

She wants out, wants to run. Moving across silt and loam through creeks blue with high in the sky, she trips and turns. This love is quick and quick and show(y). She laps the dryness of moonlight, choking on expectations greater than her blues can swallow, too saline for resolution. Moving out of the razor sharp gaze, she surrenders to the moment, surrenders movement toward or away from her target.

C chases love, not

This is not funny, she cries. She cries. Or sings. A comedy of heirs.

Seeds of love (im)plant and she carries them away in little balloons of (dis) interest. They sail backwards through the tubes of time, position themselves in forms of memory. Mesmerized by the tempo of laughs that hold up behind her teeth, beneath her breath, below her abdomen, they loosen and float on waves of wor(l/d)y scores and move into the expands of thyme.

C chases love, not knowing why or

Cold grows into a love cliché. It starts at the base of the heart (the one with a V) and climbs each side, reaching for curves that hug idea(l)s.

She is quoted spinning language, stories, bodies, webs, baby blankets, lies, wheels, airwaves, circles of ponies. She spins. Love f(r)ails to move. It raps around her shape, closes in on the waste. Love flips. A little

lies a little

C chases love, not knowing why or how she will

Drinking in the sizzle, she redirects her retention. She sings, Please baby. Pleas. The accent pirouettes off her tongue. This love(r) moves slow, slow, quick, quick, slow. The dance. Masculinity forces her back and gives up and away. I'll buy a vowel, she screams. U. How about a Y.

How about I

or O

This little love dripping letters, dropping (sp)aces, developing mean(ing). This, She sings, is not a game. It is a bold war. (Serio)us business.

C chases love not

Not a joke, this love curls around her hot strings. It burrows into her core, slides through arteries, hits roadblocks, and bounces. It morphs into a new structure with each phrase. Built on broken rules and cries, it crescendos, floods the roads of dire desire before falling into the theory of the ode.

Love tunes into a bard and calls out, Won't you be mine. And, Take me I'm ours. And, Sweet child of mine. And, Be mine tonight. She answers, Any man of mine. She sings. Cries. Draws her weapon. Drops her good.

Forgets the power(lessness) of her arms

C

C tastes ropes for gunpowder. Refines what she is looking for. For she is

Love(r) is dangerous. Swerves. She is (not) (a)lone(r). Click, click, (sha)boom(!). There are dance(r)s moving toward disregard. Her lips blush rose. Cheeks implant kisses. Holding the love, she blisters. She skirts in boots, calling to the voice of a lost (m)other. I didn't, she sings. Mean to, she cries. I'm, she says. Sorrow. Mmmm other, she tastes.

Please for. Give me.

Good-bye, she shoots.

C Chases love, not knowing who or how she will

Chasing seduction, skin drawn by metaphors or music or braided trails. She breathes in the scent of sorrow, churns in to mutter, releases in to the night black as crow. She disguises herself as glamour, as rebellion, as bottled and canned misperfection. She waits. Is a trap, ready to ring her prayers.

This love is palpable. Capable. (In)escapable. It spins on a 45. It reels on a cassette, waits to move. For word

What do you do, it asks. She is desperate not serious. She sings, Where O where. And, Why O why. And pleas. Be mine.

C Chases love, not knowing why or how she will catch

C dreams a change is gonna come. It does (not). This love looks like a newborn dream, feels like father sublime. It tastes like plastic. Like canned beans and steam. It reads like spam. She holds on tight and travels—a hag riding on proud thigh. And sighs

Laughing. Rolling. Reaching. Rocking. This love moves through her fast, settles in and storms, bolting her to rebirthed idea(l)s. She hangs in the air. Slamming into the atmosphere, cushioned by the vapor of clouds, she can no longer see as the sun sets or rises.

She (re)leases theories of love and lust and loss into the puff of a cloud and (re)coils.

She is in waiting, ready to move on or not, ready to move in and out of (re) constructed notions or emotions.

She chases

9. according to itel

holler

8. it she doesn't close

longoloid children

·asket of eggs into little

ging body is turning her

7. a realization that her

f reality

6. taker [pick a vowel]

DOG STORIES

Story 1: It is an honor to be the world's ugliest dog. Every year in California (the plastic surgery capital of the US), a contest is held that honors the world's ugliest dog's owner with a thousand dollars and a bag of publicity. Past winners of this prestigious award include Yoda, Pabst, Elwood, and three-time winner Sam (blindness a plus for Sam). While ugliness is as subjective as beauty, it can also be met with a bullet to the brain, a burlap sack and concrete block, or a simple twist of the neck. (Conversely, ugly girls are looked upon with pity whenever it is possible to look at them at all. The owners of ugly girls are never awarded a thousand dollars nor do they get any press at all for possessing such a creature.)

Story 2: Replacing a crow and a pair of geese, there is a dog sitting under a tree with a girl. She uses him as a pillow. She uses him as a friend, tells him stories about being called names that she does not understand. She is a dirty girl, the names say. A slut, they say. The dog listens, waiting for the hotdogs that will follow the sobbing. The dog listens, waiting for the girl to pull ticks, to brush his coat, to hold his muzzle in both hands and kiss his face with soft affection that travels down his spine until it reaches his tail and shakes his understanding of love and safety and sadness.

Story 3: Seventy dogs were seized from the property of a powerful League of Players star for evidence of dog fighting and animal abuse. Under the busted operation, those dogs who passed "training" to make them aggressive were allowed to live to fight. If fighting meant living. Those who refused to become aggressive enough to star in the sport selected for them were (inhumanely) destroyed. While one dog year equals seven human years of life, it is unclear how many dogs' lives are worth a single human life, as the defendant is back in the League of Players making public announcements against animal abuse and the sport of dog fighting.

Story 4: A dog loves the taste of lamb, is surrounded by small, soft-boned newborns. Their scent teasing his taste, traveling through his memory, his mouth watering. Dry processed kibble in his bowl freezing in the Midwestern February air. Dog fighting the memory of boots in ribs and the touch of human hands to love or discipline. Affection versus instinct. Processed imitation meat versus that thing he wants most. To satisfy a primordial urge to eat. To survive. To exercise his right to hunt. The scent of lanolin and milky breath and he can't take it any longer, drives his young teeth through the neck, blood flowing into his mouth. Swallowing life. He hurries to finish the carcass. Too late. There are rocks chucked at his head. He blacks out for a moment before returning to the boot that separates ribs. He slinks away, belly creating a trench in the snow. Later, he finds forgiveness, jumps into the cab of the pickup and rides to the top of the hill to a field waiting for spring. When the truck stops, he gets out to mark the field, to sniff for rabbits or squirrels. He feels a thud to the back of his head, drops to the ground, and sinks into the earth.

Story 5: A dog is a girl's best friend. If there is such a thing as a best friend or a dog.

Story 6: Either looking to have a good time or repulsed by the presence of a little lab, the puppy's owners begin to break legs one at a time. When the first leg snaps, the wailing of the pup swells. To control the noise, the mouth of the creature is glued shut, followed by the eyes and ears, just to make sure no sound escapes. After the final three limbs are broken, the still-living puppy becomes a liability. Knowing that there might be a fine or charges filed or that the body might die and begin emitting the stench of decomposition, the owners take the puppy to a nearby dumpster where it is tossed away and later dies.

Story 7: There are dogs that weave their way in and out of a life. They live and are murdered or die or escape the pull of a human life, always coming back and forth on tiny threads of that life working their way into dreams and actions and time. Resting only when the life spins in place. Reigning in rage and sorrow. Forcing terror out of the thick air surrounding (out)laws. Apparitions of love and tenderness, they cannot help but cycle and recycle through perception, waiting for it let go, waiting for it to reach for them and finally escape.

Story 8: A family visits a shelterand brings home a shepherd rescued from a puppy mill. The timid dog spends three months in the hands of gentle humans. Every day for three months she is groomed, stroked, nuzzled, fed, watered, and given boxes of treats. Her responses move from being paralyzed when touched to tail wagging and, eventually, to whining when her family leaves. After building a large fence to protect the dog and give her the opportunity to enjoy the great outdoors, the family leaves home long enough for the dog to be abducted. Her toenails are trimmed below the quick, each toe bleeding. Her teeth are filed almost to the gum line and she is placed on the soft grass of a freshly mowed lawn. She is introduced to a large male on a leash. Her abductor says things like, Sick em. And, Get er. And, Go. And, Fight. As the abductor boots her in the side a growl brews from deep within the large male morphing into a series of staccato barks. He lunges forward, teeth closing down on her muzzle, ripping away the freshly groomed fur. She cowers as teeth clench her neck. The abductor pulls back the large male, frees the bitch. She stands and begins to growl, nips at the male, her gums slipping away. The abductor frees the male to clench down on her neck once more, this time there is nothing or nobody to temper his rage.

Story 9: There are dogs who bark too loud, too often. They chase raccoons and squirrels and warn their owner of a pack of coyotes approaching the hen house. Every night there is a routine of barking and chasing and protecting, because this is what the owner expects and what the dogs are driven by nature to do. There are neighbors who are certain that the owner is herself a bitch, neighbors who dislike the sound of barking. There are cops who draw imaginary lines across property boundaries. There are neighbors who take things into their own hands with rifles and rat poison and heavy machinery. There are dogs who disappear and dogs who are captured and dogs who never barked but eat large doses of green pellets manufactured to make rodents slowly bleed to death.

Story 10: There is a dog. One that rides on the tank of a motorcycle. One that rides in the car of a young girl searching. One that is abandoned, given to a farm and a father figure or a mother lost in madness. One that disappears. One that climbs a fence, front legs holding down barbed wire, back legs stepping up each row of wire. Front legs struggling to reach the ground as barbs sink into stomach flesh and then the hide of the back legs and the front legs, reaching for the ground, reaching for the girl, reaching for the shelter of the shade tree where the tangled dog was once pillow and friend. Legs and emotion reaching. Barbs digging deeper, slicing skin, working their way into meat but not into anything vital like a heart or liver or soul. The dangling dog dangling waits for rescue or death. Barbs digging, prying open threads of meat. Just waiting. And nobody knows. Nobody cares. Nobody saves the dog, sun pushing hard against his dark coat. Tongue reaching for water. Memory reaching for time. And nobody knows. Nobody rescues the accidental dog until death slowly seeps in, shutting down one organ at a time. A kidney one day, a liver the next, until the heart can no longer work alone, until hope fails and there is nothing left but a carcass decaying in the autumn sun.

Story 11: Before Bob Barker wanted your pet spade or neutered, there were dogs having puppies because that's what dogs did. The bitch had a litter of fourteen little brown coydogs, canines that would never make a pet, that would surely terrorize livestock and children. Thirteen of the puppies were tossed into a burlap sack and taken to the river where they floated and sunk and resurfaced, catfish biting on burlap until the sack came undone and the bodies freed to sink or wash up and decay. The fourteenth puppy was kept as an experiment. It learned to herd cattle, chase foxes and raccoons or opossums away from the chicken house, to comfort crying children or women (and men), and to sit, heal, and fetch a stick or ball.

Story 12: It is legal to shoot your own dog so long as it is not done in a manner that causes excessive suffering. It is legal to ask a vet to kill your dog via lethal injection, even if your dog is happy, healthy, and has not committed a crime nor been tried and convicted by a jury of its peers. It is illegal to shoot a girl, even if she is suffering, homely, or has a broken bone.

Story 13: A dog is man's best friend until time comes to pull the trigger.

CC Stat

CC on an scenic drive named after a river that flows into the Mississippi; she drives Sugar Daddy's truck with 75.3 of his dollars and one of Sweet Daddy's bucks. She carries a list and a wish.

Town 1 smells like dust and diesel.[1]

CC drives away with 7 bags of popcorn, a pickle in a paper sack, 2 new versions of history.

In between the slight towns CC sings about country roads, sings story about Delta Dawn.[2]

Roadkill lining the ditch. CC stops, tries to identify the unidentifiable, guesses dog or wolf or bear or baby bigfoot for the large one and squirrel or monkey for the little one. She sits in the recliner, kicks the tire, lifts the recliner into the pickup.

Town 2 tastes like corn silk and oil. Residents ring, Hey girl. And, Got a buck.[3]

CC hangs a fetish around her neck, a series of turquoise nuggets circling her wrist, a dozen corndogs in foam boxes.

In between, the colors of tractors indicate status and class, privilege and poverty. Tractor colors preach history. Cite politics.[4]

---

1. Population: 802
Stands offering Native American goods: 28
Stands offering country décor: 39
Number of traffic accidents: 1 (not CC)

2 Roadkill: 3 raccoons, 1 skunk, 1 deer, 1 fox, 2 unidentified carcasses
Visible Trash: 1 cardboard box, 1 Hardee's cup, 2 McDonald's bags, 1 recliner in fair shape, 1 tire
Flowers in bloom: Goldenrod, ragweed, asters
The lilies are spent

3. Vendors selling original paintings: 2
Vendors selling crafts: 72
Vendors selling corndogs: 12
Number of stands offering vegetarian alternatives: 0

4. Roadkill: 2 cats, a family of 4 raccoons, a buck and doe, 2 squirrels
Stop signs: 1
Farmers on green tractors: 4
Farmers on red tractors: 12

CC (re)writes the story of roadkill. The cats out to party with lilies and tigers and tales. The raccoons part of a semi-religious cult, victims of suicide and pacts. The deer fighting urges. Squirrels with bodies ahead of their actions, she thinks. CC blows off the stop sign, waves to farmers on red tractors, sits in a bathtub sitting on the roadside but cannot lift it.

>Town 3 is closing in on itself; it feels like thyme on the tongue, tastes like a punch.[5]

CC buys a deep fried chicken, pays 2 kids 1 dollar to serve a stray dog.

>In between a mantra slams against CC's skull; it can't break through but the vibrations are telling her something.[6]

The ditch holding death, holding secrets. CC stops to study the large dog, sees Pyrenees in the curve of the tail and dew claws, sees coyote or wolf in the coat, something in the open eye—it is speaking in codes.

>Town 4 reminds her of Minnie Pearl and Grandpa Jones.[7]

CC buys an old sunlamp, one that says it is so safe you can sleep under it, one that looks like a spotlight. The box is torn and sticky with mouse shit, inside the lamp seems new. CC buys a rock for Sugar Daddy, an iron skillet for Sweet Daddy, a bottle of Avon for Hot Momma. Wishes she could buy something other than flowers for Running Love.

>In between, she disregards little incantations—sounds from which direction she cannot tell.[8]

---

5. Current population: 559 (down 28.1% from twenty years ago today)
Total number of vendors: 70 (67 local)
Number of stands offering dried weeds spray painted mauve and gold: 7
Number of stray dogs: 1

6. Roadkill: 1 small canine (missing head), 1 large canine (possible coydog or chupacabra), 1 turkey
Number of businesses: 1 country craft store/fuel station/produce market/hair salon/(not so) quick lube service/livestock feed store
Number of homes with goats and chickens on the front porch: 2

7. Population: 245
Number of stray cats: 65
Number of vendors selling goods commonly found at yard sales or in garbage dumps: 30

8. Number of businesses: 1 (Cooter's Transmission and Engine Repair. Cooter refuses to do hair. Gives away produce.)
Number of road signs: 17, all No Trespassing

CC disregards a pair of Do Not Pass signs and 21 pot holes. She remembers how Sugar Daddy told her she was a good girl, how he said she was his own girl, his only daughter. How she was his and that he loved her and handed her a wad of ones.

Town 5 sounds like a broken Mayberry. There is no Sherriff, no Fife.[9]

CC stops, selects a stray dog (a beagle mix), scoops it up and rides.

In between a bond forms.[10]

CC and Beagle stop on the roadside to pee. CC pees on grass, Beagle on a tire.

Town 6 smells like gun smoke, tastes like soy dust.[11]

CC and Beagle eat catfish dinners on paper. CC leaves bones. Beagle leaves nothing. Beagle drinks water from a puddle, CC Pepsi from a bottle, which reminds her of how Sweet Daddy used to take her to the Mite Market and buy bagged peanuts and put them in the soda bottles. She remembers how they fizzed, tasted like the past, how the peanuts and soda turned into each other, borrowed space and separated. CC thinks about Sweet Daddy's gait, about how his hands have morphed into spotted hides crawling across bone. She rubs the fetish, pats Beagle, drinks hard.

---

9. Average household income: $12, 459.13 before and after federal taxes
Number of stray dogs: 6
Number of living stray cats: 1
Number of stray cats eaten by stray dogs: undetermined
Porta potties: 0

10. Number of vehicles without tires rusting in yards: 21 cars, 9 trucks, 3 tractors, 1 combine
Number of children on bicycles: 5
Number of buzzards circling: 3
Number of crows eating roadkill: 8

11. Number of residents who regularly engage in illegal hunting and fishing: 71
Number of residents who have not been to a doctor in more than 5 years: 81
Number of residents who have never seen a dentist: 97
Number of residents who will suffer a heart attack or stroke before the age of 55: 74

C BABY

Hot Momma and Sugar Daddy ride buggy to town. Sugar Daddy wearing leather bibs and an oversized gold ring with a cat's eye. Hot Momma tilts a head full of Aquanet, floats a table cloth dress. Horse A and Horse B pull the buggy, swat flies with tails, ignite little tugs against reigns, lick bits.

I lost a baby, says Hot Momma, rubbing mulberry on her lips.

My baby, asks Sugar Daddy.

No, Sweet Daddy's.

Where's my baby, says Sugar Daddy, punching a hornet.

Dead.

Why dead.

It was born wrong.

Born wrong, he asks.

Wrong side out. Heart pumping in the air. You know, wrong.

What'd you do to it.

Put it down by the riverside.

To die.

It died before it bounced away.

What happened to it.

Fish ate its eyes.

Why the river.

The river swallowed the bundle whole. It was winter. The ground was frozen. The coyotes were gone.

The coyotes are never gone. Where's Sweet Daddy's baby.

Gone.

Where.

It rolled out of the buggy way back.

Today.

Yesterday.

Evening.

Morning, I think.

Let's look for it.

No.

Let's look.

No.

We should go back.

No. It's long gone. It was just a baby.

Just a baby.

I can have another. Do you wanna have another, Sugar.

Baby.

Yes.

No.

Please.

No, they're making you look bad, stretching you out like an old balloon, you're falling down, looking like leather, like your eyes are sitting in navels, like your lips have been stretched around a tire or watermelon.

Please.

No, it is too hard on you. Too hard for you.

Pleas.

No, you keep losing them.

Only a few.

A dozen.

Come on.

No. Your eggs are spoiled.

Fine. Go back.

What for.

I want Sweet Daddy's baby, says Hot Momma.

No.

Why, she wanders.

Too far back.

I know where it is.

How, Sugar Daddy is wandering.

I left it on a fence post.

I thought it fell out of the buggy.

(Horse A jumps toward Horse B.)

Hot Momma screams.

Relax, tosses Sugar Daddy. Horse A is just afraid of tiger lilies.

Hot Momma puts her head in a basket and fills it with regrets.

Sugar Daddy pulls reigns right and right around. Quit whining, he smacks.

Hot Momma, rests her head against Sugar Daddy's bear chest. She sings lullabies about bed bugs or baskets in trees or parsley and thyme.

Sugar Daddy belts reigns against horse hide, forms clicks in his cheek, drives.

Sunrise tracks sun down, finds Hot Momma pickin banjo.

Sugar Daddy, grinning, Where O where can that baby be. He stops the buggy. Smiles at the ditch. Taps Hot Momma.

Hot Momma smears eyes, becomes raccoon, touches Sugar Daddy where it counts.

A John Wayne Hero/Sonofabitch/Sinner/Lover

When they find C Baby, he's wearing his
best Saturday night shirt and cowboy
hat.

C Baby is covered in dust and blood,
tears and crow. Beneath the filth there is
checkered skin, pale and sun burned or
black and white or blue and black.
Sugar Daddy swaddles her in his shirt,
holds her close to his body. He says,
What a girl.

Baby C says nothing, refuses to cry.
Rubbing the crow and blood off her
face, Sugar Daddy kisses her forehead.
What a girl, he repeats.

Hot Momma tries to take the baby, but
Sugar Daddy turns her away. Leave her
alone, he says.

But she's mine, cries Hot Momma.
You lost her. She doesn't want you.

Give her here.

She's mine. I'll take care of here.

You're a man; you don't know how.

He sits in a leather recliner
thinking about everybody
who wants his
money.

He tells CC to take the cash,
to burn it, to feed it to the
river.

He says, Don't touch the cash.

His eyes matter.
Not wanting anybody to
misinterpret weakness, he
shuts them, pretends to
sleep before
drifting

a way

rage brewing brewing rage rage rage brewing growing

rage rage growing brewing rag

rage rage rage growing into rage brewing rage

moving into rage coursing through rage

and rage and rage brewing growing

rage rage rage rage brewing

coursing rage coursing

Licking C Baby's face clean, Sugar
Daddy says, I know better than you.

Hot Momma, doing her best Marilyn
Monroe, Please, let me have her.

No, says Sugar Daddy, rubbing snuff
on the baby's burns.

Pursing her lips and softening her voice,
Hot Momma pleas,
Pleeeeease, Sugar. Please.

Placing his hat on the baby, Sugar
Daddy turns his back on Hot
Momma.

Hot Momma gets in the buggy.

Good, says Sugar Daddy. Fine.

Buried beneath a hat, Baby C sings,
My heroes have always been
cowboys.

Sugar Daddy collecting.
Trading.
Growing.

Sugar Daddy visits Sweet Daddy.
There's a baby, he says.

Holding out his hand, Sweet Daddy
shakes, says, Congratulations.

I'm here to see if Running Love
wants to move in and take care of the
baby.

He is thick, his lines
broad, his fingers like
little Popeye arms. He
is pink on the outside,
the valleys of his creases
white in the morning,
dark at sundown, thick
with oil and dirt. After
a mule kicks his face, he
buys 10 false teeth. Later
invests in a pair of gold
caps to top fillings. He
makes sure to get gold,
gives his cavities status.

He no longer controls his body.   It refuses.
He no longer controls CC.

                                                She refuses.

Working for a living, a legacy, a nickel a day, a week, a year.
Or a quarter. Depending on the slant, Sugar Daddy carries
50- or 60- or 100-pound bags of concrete mix to make
the roads his children ride to the sale barn, to school, to
the wooden sheds where their friends share moonshine or
homemade wine.

He paves the roads his grandchildren travel to fast food
joints and marts full of things they believe in. The roads he
drives his first car on, a car purchased off the gains from
trading $5 mules for $20 mares, from trading glass jars for
gold teeth and pocket watches, from trading 159 furs for
cash in a single season.

What's the matter with me, he says to the
doctor.
Can't ya fix me, he says.
When can I go home, he says to Hot Momma.
When can I go home, he says to CC.
Soon, they lie.
If that old woman Running Love was around, I
bet she'd take care of me, he says.

A story.   A teller.

He cultivates tales of fights. Braggs
how he beat this one or that one
for stealing a dog or horse, for
spitting in his driveway, for looking
at Hot Momma a little too long or
a little bit wrong.

He swears and swears, They
deserved it.

How he'd done the world a favor.

How his kind of justice was best.

I'd like to nail his bag to a tree and
give him a butter knife, he says
about a man who raped his own
newborn daughter.

You know, Baby C, he
says. When I was a kid,
we ate eggs, if we ate.

When I was a kid, Pa
butchered my pet cow.

When I was a kid, he
says. CC, can you hear
me. Are you listening.

Hot Momma was a
looker, he says. She
could sing and dance
and play the fiddle.

She could do things.

they say.

they say

They are like animals, he says.

and say

He grows corn,
cattle,   and tales.

and say

People say things like:

they say

He owns half the county.

The old bastard is a crook.

He sold me a lame horse.

say

Fetch my
rifle, he says.

He cheats at the card table.

Fetch my wallet.

He cheats at the sale barn.

He's crocked as they come.

say

He has a basement full of gold
bars and army rifles.

He has things, has done things.

The old bastard.

things

I have to go home,
he says.
They are crazy
around here.
I have to
go
home

they say

GIRLFRIENDS

Borderline is a charge gazing from behind wayfarers. I feel for pulse beneath a symphony or lace. Dancing to the jingle of crosses and chains. Tapping. Rapping. I say, Sing. She bounces. I say, Talk to me. She snaps gum. I don't have to say, Dance. She is dance. Stop playing (with my heart), I say. She flashes and shoots away, dusting me with desire. I chase her vapor, but it disappears as my craving for her crescendos.

Reaching for me, Lucky Star, tangles my hair and hopes in bangles. I say, Love. She says nothing. She touches my face. Smiles. Sweet and sweat and silent notes slip between her teeth. She says, You must be mine. And, Make everything. Alright. I try to comb her hair, but she grapevines away. Come back, I say. Lucky in love. Lucky to be alive. Lucky to be. Mine. Lucky to have moved out of range.

Dress You Up In My Love says, You've got style. I look down at denim and dust, at frays and chains. I say, Velvet kisses. But she's floating away, abandoning the beat. I move all over, all over, but she does not see. I imagine her riding the wave of my tempo, laughing at a missed beat, but she has dissipated.

I find Like a Virgin surging on stage. I slip into her white. She says, Oooo o o. Spins away. Cake, I say. She rolls on the floor, slipping. Beneath a veil, she looks up, silently says it all, pulses to a beat. Heartbeat, she says. Feel it, she asks. I turn away. Say nothing. Afraid to consume the offering.

Baby goes all the way on the cover of the *Rolling Stone*. Tasting ink, melting text. She compares (im)perfection to im(perfection) and wins. I call to her, but she cannot hear me. Lust, I try to say. So I say nothing. I don't want to know what's in the shadows, but I keep looking. I can't help it, I say. She cannot speak with words, uses imagery to do things. To do everything. Almost everything. Her art a donation to my ache. Is it reproduction or the real thing, I wander. She is offended or hurt. Baby goes all the way away.

I see Who's That Girl, drifting through spring. She reaches in, kisses my heart, the flavor of her mouth cruising through air, through my veins into the bends and recesses of my curves. My body tries to run and flow faster, but she stops me. She says, You can't get up. I don't move. She skips. I don't move. When she turns, I begin to wonder. I want her to stop me, but she doesn't.

True Blue bathes in soundwaves. Spins like a record, tasting nostalgia, the top of the top of her head chemically faded to almostvirgin white. She calls me True Love. Smokes, O baby. Other girls follow her, kicking haughtiness at my face. True, they say. Blue, they say. Baby, they say. I melt in the seat of a Cadillac, fade into leather. Stuck in a crevice with quarters, petrified fries, and a crushed fortune cookie.

Like a Prayer smacks like a child. I hear her voice, but she isn't speaking. She calls me. Please, I say. Pleas. I pray. She disappears, slinks into bars with a lover. Not this one. I feel the burn of her fire, the heat of her cross and ascend into sleep. When I wake, it is all about drama and gyrations. It is the end of the beginning.

Do you believe, says Express Yourself. I don't answer. Come on, she says. I continue working, distracted by dirty boys in brass chains. xXxpress yourself, she begs. I turn but fail to (re)connect with her rhythm. She dissolves into creamy satin, her lips blushing against darkness, moving and silent. I touch but cannot reach her. She affects me and fades.

The sun rises on Ray of Light. I know, if I look away, she will liquefy into a line that exi(s)ts like babies coloring in the sun. She begins to fade behind time, behind blurred sketches or clouds or locks. She sounds mechanical, tinny and tiny. Slow down, I say. I feel, she says. Like, she says. I feel. I say, I, too, feel. She's moving too fast. She's flying. She escalates, recesses, disappears. Stop, I say. It is too late.

The Power of Good-Bye splashes against me. Darkness moving across her face, she brings the sea inland, washes over fields, over me, over and over. A runaway lover, the sky fits heaven and I drop at her feet. I say, Is this a forbidden love or erotica. She says things like, Human is animal. And, Swim. And, Love don't live here. And, That's the power of good-bye. Love or bust, I write on her satin. Desire or die, I smoke in the sky. Good or bye. I have lipstick on my heart.

There is no good in bye.

C

Hot Momma, eyes little mouths surrounded by puffs of lips, lashes biting on sorrow, lets loose of Baby C who no longer wants held or loved or to go shopping at Uncle Ed's. A baby no longer a baby. A language tosser and distorter of meanings or intentions or love.

Baby C tired of Hot Momma's (s) mothering. C is NOT a baby. Indy C. Any thing C. Missed at understanding, C. C moving on, moving up, moving away, moving. C shouts what Hot Momma distorts. C barks.

Hot Momma, crying, Come back. Begging, Mine.

Baby C, pounding, Mine. Tossing, Stop.

Hot Momma circling Baby, herding, hoarding, Stop, she says. Baby C, slow down. Please.

Baby C shatters the circle. Kicks at the herding. You are not mine, she pushes.

Hot Momma reaches out. Pleas. Holds onto Baby C's breath, absorbs the action and tense. Rides words. Wishes for baby Baby days. Says things like, Remember. And, When. And, You. And, Loved. And, Me.

Baby C punches air, I can't. Breathe. And, You stared this. And, I will end this. And, Where is my breath. And, Where is it. And, Stop. Leave me a-lone.

Hot Momma tosses air at Baby C. Have it, she says. Just have it. I know.

Baby C reaches out, grabs the breeze and looks away. She says things like, Mine. And, Get. And, Out. And, Of MY life. She sweeps little disregards toward the circle.

Hot Momma flings, I'm miserable.

Baby C spits, Able. You missed, she says.

Hot Momma falling to the floor, howls.

Hot Momma says, You can't kill Baby. I killed her before she was born. I killed Baby.

Hot Momma says nothing. And neverminds. She places a wrist on her forehead.

Baby C roars, I killed Baby.

Baby C says, I killed Baby. She was mine.

C says, Good. And, Bye. And prays to gods she does not believe in.

DREAM

Sweet Daddy in Stasis

The feeling comes
like floodwaters
dancing down
the Mississippi.
It surrounds him,
pulls him down,
holds his head
underwater, waiting
for him to fight
or flee. waiting for
him.

He tracks his
decision to higher
ground where he
kneels, reaches for
the long steel arms
of an unfelt lover
he knows well from
dream bursts of
delivery and dread.

As the engine
reaches him,
the sound is an
April wind or an
old Dodge on
new Main or an
angry semi on the
interstate. As it
approaches him,
he is doubled over
like a rag on a
tightrope—he is an
ancient nag hacking.

Maddog and blood
as deep as
overcast
night. Sour
as grain rotting in a
field full of f(l)ood.

As it nears, it feels
like a debt collector,
like a drought in
July or June, like
thin skin frying in
a skillet, fat stores
snapping against
the last drops of
water. It feels as
sleek as a storm as
fake as a funeral
arrangement or
forecast, like the
meeting of now
and never, like the
clash of a single-
celled contradiction.

When it reaches
him it looks empty
as its essence
evaporates into hot
waves of autumn
air swimming
toward the sun,
leaving nothing but
thought shadows
lurking.

Behind walls of
white. Clouds cast.
Against a crayon
blue sky.

The lovely monster
moans, the sound
of the whistle is
silence absorbed
by the scream
of steel scraping
against itself. The
slick metal shines
cold, then turns hot
as fast as rolling
numbers on a filling
station board, as
fast as a bucket of
luck tossed into the
air.

It smells like
progress, like
passion faded into
a leathery prune,
like oil, like life or
death.

Hacking, his mind
calculates losses
and gains and losses
and probabilities
and speculates
the likelihood of
luck or lack of
luck, the use of
steel horseshoes.
Lucky Charms.

Pros. Cons.
Swirl in a twister
pushing out on,
spiraling toward the
core of his tired
skull.

The blind eye
appears blank
behind the socket.
He cannot connect
to an empty
current. He is no
fawn, no squirrel,
not a nut.

As the hind feet
of roadkill kick his
bleeding mouth,
he rolls away from
peace, away from
the snorting engine,
away from leisure,
into a bank where
one season's grass
grows through that
of another. Snake
eyes staring at him,
he slithers through
his choice, up the
hill to his rusty
pickup, his own

denial
already
growing
discontent.

FIND(H)ER

When I find

    her, she

       is float

          ing elec

            tric eels ligh

               ting up li

                    quid locks of d

                         itch

weed

wrapped firm

    ly a

      round her

         wrists,   tethering

                her   tongue.

Her

eye

 s say

   things like,

       Come closer.

       And, I lov

          e you. And,   Give

                         me

                         your

                         breath.

HOLIDAY

She pulls the tab on the indoor formula 9-Lives beef dinner with garden vegetables, because she's spent the past eight weeks indoors, because she's wasted four lives, because three lives have been stolen, because she's been murdered, because she can't get back her wasted, stolen lives, because the murderer was too busy blinking to see the bullet go into the wall beside her head, because she's an actress, one who can fall like an elk with heatstroke, quiver, hold still, roll her eyes back, and stare, unblinking regardless of how bad it burns. And she can hold it long enough to fool a murderer with Mr. Magoo eyeballs and a sobbing barrel.

She pulls the tab on the 9-Lives cat food because, really, she has no choice, she wasted four of her lives, because when she should have said no, she said yes, because the stretch marks wrap around her like rubber bands, because the marks look like a tiger opened her up, because not even duct tape can pull them together, because she threw up for three months and ate for three months and threw up for three-point-four or more months, because they said push and she pushed, because she pushed when she would have rather been sleeping or doped up on a shot or drip or pill that makes a person dull or unresponsive or bitter and mouthy.

She pulls the tab on the indoor formula 9-Lives, because it has garden vegetables, because she remembers her own garden, a wall of plants pushing down metal cages, tomatoes buried in foliage, remembers working her way around daddy longlegs to pick fruits that worms had already marked with eye sockets, how she wasted so many tomatoes, how the leaves turned her skin into little raised bumps that itched like wool or fleas or fire ants, how, when she showered, the yellow tomato dust stayed on the washrag, how she found mushrooms growing just yards from her garden, how she learned to identity a morel, but not well enough, because she fried a toxic impersonator, because it tasted like a real morel with flour and salt and pepper and grease or wax.

She pulls the tab on the 9-Lives, because she's spent the last weeks in a musty motel room, a hole without sheets or maid service, a hole with a hole in the wall, a hole sealed with a washrag and duct tape, because there is no service on the mountaintop, because there are no fast food joints within walking distance, because she's wasted four lives and had three stolen, because one of the lives was taken away by a big-headed bear, because she fell for his soft fur chest, because he chased away the other outwardly aggressive bears, because his teeth were so white, so shiny, because she's always liked the way bears walk and smoke Swisher Sweets.

She pulls the tab, because she's had three lives stolen, because she had a lump on her gum, because the lump was just an infection, because it was just a lump, because it was nothing to worry about, because it was not a thing, because the lump grew and it was just a persistent infection, just a bigger piece of nothing, because it kept growing like a hungry child, like a river in a flood, because it filled her lip and her nasal passages and pushed one eye shut before it became anything at all, because it was nothing before it was too late to save her face, because the surgeon wanted to make sure he got it all, because a face, after all, is only for the superficial, only a luxury.

She pulls the tab on the beef dinner, because she wasted four of her lives, because she remembers a calf name Sirloin, because the calf grew into a bull, because he was a longhorn, because she'd seen the vet dehorn a calf once and she saw the brain peering through the skullhole, because the other calf balled and bled, because the other calf sounded like death, because she didn't want Sirloin butchered, because longhorns are exotic and people say things like O. And, Awe. And, Wow. Because Sirloin was short tempered, because she just wanted to love him, because she thought she was much faster and Sirloin much slower or nicer or much calmer or much more reasonable. She just wanted to love. For him to love.

She pulls the tab on the indoor formula, because she's forgotten what the outdoors is like, how salty the ocean tastes, how it burns her nose when she does summersaults underwater, how it feels to have a grouper slide by her leg as she swims too far out beyond the reach of the lifeguards that don't patrol the beaches on little islands that sound like Anna Marie and Longboat Key, because she had so many lives stolen, because when she was driving down Alligator Alley she ran out of fuel, because the man in the pickup smiled and said, Need some fuel, girly. Because she was less afraid of a stranger in the dark than spirits of gators or men or history, because she was blazing tired and the mosquitoes had filled her Pinto, because the bites were swelling like little tumors, because the fuel was worth more than the vehicle or cassettes in the tape deck. Because there was no Sugar and old men couldn't really hurt girls—she kept telling herself, reaching for her scars.

She pulls the tab on the indoor formula 9-Lives beef dinner with garden vegetables, because she's spent the last weeks indoors, because she's wasted four lives, because three lives have been stolen, because she's been murdered, because she can't get back her wasted or stolen lives but she (re)imagines them, because she dated a gun named Shooter, because Shooter was a chemist, because he stole anhydrous from her father figure, because he exchanged bucks for the pseudoephedrine of desperate parents, because he smelled like decay before he was dead, because she was a sucker for tiger tattoos, because she loved his long hair and grayness, because one might manufacture love if one can manufacture drugs and houses and roller coasters, because she said yes when she should have said no.

O Sister, Where Art Thou

Born into captivity, she slept in a metal box for nearly a year, locked away. She sang, Don't bring me down, while cinematic sounds of others playing and fighting, panting and running, living and dying, frying in the heat of July, drifted into her dreams from outside the box. She could hear the soft sounds of feet hitting hardened earth, breath and breeze entering through corroded sideslits. And she thought, Try a little tenderness, but nobody tried—nobody was tender. The outside came in glimpses as the door was opened to toss in a bowl or bone, the green grass of home glinting in the distance, autumn's grackle grays, and snow(less) metallics taunted her.

```
Xxxxxx Xxxxxx,
[from then to
now]

XX of [my box
number minus
10] [my road],
[my city], [my
state] died at
home [a few
days ago]. He
was a member
of…. He worked
for…. and was
well-respected
for…. He is
survived by
[one son and
a whole bunch
of other fam-
ily members
who drive too
fast]. Services
will be held
[at the local
funeral home].
Donations can
be made to….
```

(s/t)he(y)

      define chicken seed

           inside stresslines form out of used speech and little (dis)
                                        regards
                  inside the baby doesn't cry

When she got yard privileges, she ate up her parole by fighting
with cats and chickens. Each time she was locked back up, she
cried, They're hanging me tonight.

The first dog I know is a black and tan named Ford after a mechanical mess that
rests rusting in Sweet Daddy' pasture. He lies on a concrete step and wags a tail.
Not all of the dogs have tails.

Not all of the dogs have tales. Ford sits in a photograph his black grayed, Hot
Momma at her most beautiful disappearing into a pinkish pale, their youth fading
backwards. Photopaper by Kodak; Kodak claiming Hot Momma, claiming Ford,
tainting the memory.

She was brought to me in the back of a pick-up, only plywood
between her feet and the axel, between her feet and defeat, between her feet and freedom. She was afraid of the shed, worried
about me, fearful of the foreign stench and cried, Country roads,
take me home.

Transferred from one prison to the next, she awaited release without ever having been reformed. The wolf look in her soul, her
unwillingness to be touched, to look into my eyes, left me uneasy
as I stood tall, took command, shouted orders. Ee-evil woman.
What's goin on. Be patient, a change is gonna come.

I, at four or three or something-point-fiveorso, am unaffected when Ford dies of
old age. Sugar Daddy burns him atop a pile of busted tires.

Next is a tough guy named Badger.

           the cattle are lowing
          their calves are all gone

outside there is a tomcat who can't afford a nut chopper or wormer so he sprays a leg and gets a boot to the fat head, so he sprays a flowerbed and gets the hose, so he carries around little white hitchhikers in his gut and on his ass, they wave in the breeze, they wave when there is no breeze

Her freedom pending, she cried, Justice for all, clawed concrete, gnawed at wood, dreamed in the scent of the call of the wild and bleeding blades of grass.

inside lines of stress are widened by unused speech
inside the baby bed cools
years later the baby's bed is hot with rage

```
Old Bastard,
[lived too damn
long]

O. B. of [my
box number
minus 10] [my
road], [my
city], [my
state] died
outside his
home giving
orders [a few
days ago]. He
was an out-
standing member
of…. He worked
for…. and was
well-respected.
He is survived
by [one son and
a whole bunch
of other fam-
ily members].
Services will
be held.
```

inside at night there are the sounds of footsteps tearing through the attics, stomping in the yard, singing at the woods, voices in the kitchen and lots—house settling, hippies party-ing, goddamned kids causing trouble, probably trying to steal
shit

chicken egg, chicken, chicken egg
chicken, chicken egg, chicken

TheIR

                  inside the lines deepen as muscles tightened around them

                        squinting, glaring, staring, searing, smearing

outside the sun hardens the skin around those lines

      She was long like a pink Cadillac, sleek when she snuck or hunted.
      She was one ear down and one to go. Her front legs much taller
      than the back ones. She looked like she'd been built one piece at
      a time. She was long tall Sally in the front, Lola in the back. Hot
      Momma would have called her a mess, would have told her to
      straighten up, to have some dignity, to shake it a little when she
      walked.

               inside Lincoln Logs and Tinker with Toys grow a dusty moss
                            inside the baby is wormy

    Ten days after she was brought to me, I set her free. She was born
    to run, born to be wild.

Badger loves to run. He follows Sugar Daddy's green pickup from one farm to
the next, a ten-mile trip. Running, his long fur flows backwards, tongue falling
from side to side, his dustwake rolling into that of tire tread. On the way home,
he rides inside the bed while I sit on a hub. Both of us float on wind currents
and love, collecting ticks. At home, Badger forms a conga line and gets a rock in
the side.

      chicks riding conveyer belts
      into the mouths of boxes
      into the mouths of grinders
      little legs kicking
      peeping speeds up, broken heartbeats
      silence

                    inside plaster falls, riding down the inside of walls on
                              dislodged chunks of hope
                         inside the baby is away, a stranger

Badger chases raccoons, skunks, vehicles. When outsiders come, he nips at their
mirrors and chews holes in their tires. The arrivals keep their doors locked and
their windows up. They wait for someone to see what they want.

          these belts carry more than chicks
          grind more than meat

     She took to freedom humming, I believe I can fly. She took to
     freedom like an aphid to autumn, like a web on a wave of air, like
     memory on time, like thyme bees' breath, like breath on a lie.

               inside things fly like the fur and words or scenes they are to
                    never repeat—ever—never ever ever, things fly like plates
                         and speech on lightning bolts or unintentional births or
                    infants inside out, and sometimes, just once, an accidental
                                                                       bullet

          without the chicken
          there is no egg
          without the bitch
          there is no

There are dogs Sugar Daddy trades for horse tack or guns or other dogs. There
are dogs who are worth a damn and those as worthless as tits on a boar.

     The freedom was in the fight.

                    inside desire hides beneath furniture, beneath blankets,
               underneath afghans   when car tires crackle against the
                    gravel drive, when dogs bark at strangers, when the door
                    opens and someone hollers, hey, or anybody home, or boo,
               desire's voice catches in a throat or dream catcher and cannot
                                                                       escape

These are the battles she won: squirrel, squirrel, rabbit, rat, rat, rabbit, raccoon, coyote, coydog, coyote, coyote, coy dog, chicken, chicken, duck, duck, goose. Ain't it a shame. She was a super hunter, a super freak. She was super.

> inside inside there is a reason or a secret or a reason that is
> not so secret a reason
> inside the baby is out

Freedom was running a mile east or north or south or a fraction of a kill-o-meter west.

> the cattle are frantic
> the calves are all gone

There is Lass, named for a Hollywood dog who never kills a lamb or hunts for raccoons or gets shot square in the head or in a field right in the kisser.

> inside words swirl in little minds in big-headed ways: worth-
> less, worthless, worth less, worth less than…worth less than
> a pile of shit or a shotgun shell or a hooker on Adams, worth
> less than the air she breathes, goddamnedworthlessfucking-
> whore

what is a little cockerel's value

lovelie

> the cattle are all balling
> their calves are all gone

> inside the baby is tucked away in the anger, there is no crib,
> there is no bed, the baby is tucked away in the anger

Her mistakes: old man with large stick, chicken, chicken, duck, duck, goose. First mistake is the worst. First mistake landed my brown-eyed girl in a ring of fire.

```
               Dirty John
               [born one day,
               died another]

               D. J. of [my
               box number
               minus 10] [my
               road], [my
               city], [my
               state] died of
               a heart attack
               [a few days
               ago]. He was
               an outstand-
               ing member of….
               He worked for
               years and was
               [surprised at
               his own death]
               … He was well-
               respected for….
               [and then
               there's the
               other side]. He
               is survived by
               several indi-
               viduals who
               quickly settle
               the estate.
               Services will
               be held [once
               they all arrive
               and start bury-
               ing and burn-
               ing things they
               disregard].
```

Badger bites an preacher, sinking his long white man shredders deep into the preacher's rumproast. Lifemoney starts falling out of his tight ass. Chickens pecking at pennies and quarters, the sows chasing him down scooping up gold bars and wads of greenbacks. The Preacher limps for a week with an iodine red ham covered by butterflies.

without the egg
there is no chicken

familie

outside Sugar Daddy tosses the runts into the pile—a mixture of shit and straw, afterbirth and dead piglets, all fair game for dog food until it is spread onto the field—they can't be saved, says Sugar Daddy, there are things, very bad things, wrong with them, if we save them, they will die anyway, if we save them we will all go to the poorhouse

After being granted collarless, penless freedom, she anticipated every morning on the front step, her long face pointed upwards, one ear listening, perched high above her head, the other cowering, pulling her down, down, down. She waited for me to greet her, feed her, pat her skullcap, but when I tried to stroke her muzzle or hug her, gravity got her by that low down ear and forced her to the ground, four feet in the air, whining as if I were the one who'd wiped the smile off her face, as if I were the one who'd kicked the fun out of her. Her's was a bleeding love wrapped in the purple haze of her past.

the cattle are low, low, low, low, low
the calves are all gone

```
Xoo Oxx [born
too soon, died
too late]

X. O. of [my
box number
minus 10] [my
road], [my
city], [my
state] died of
a heart attack
[a few days
ago]. He was
[not] an out-
standing member
of [society].
He was [not]
well-respected
for [anything].
He is survived
by several in-
dividuals who
want nothing
more than to
quickly settle
the estate.
Services are
pending.
```

When Badger is hit by a car, I watch Hot Momma begin to spin. She cries, he he he he he he like hiccups or laughs or something concrete gray that I don't understand and mistake for something else like death or laws about speeding on dirt roads.

my-stake

> inside the ceiling cracks, Sugar Daddy and Hot Momma fill the empty space, paint over the mending and smile like nothing happened

> Her mistake: Trusting a masquerader, a maniac, who invited her to dinner, who fed her table scraps on a manic Monday, who was a sweet talkin guy, who walked by and said, Baby come on over. And she did. She went over and over. She couldn't help herself. His hands mesmerized her. His offerings sweet.

During the Badger era, there is Shebang the hunter who is only temporary because she can really fetch a buck at the flea market or raccoon trials or somewhere exotic like Missouri. Parents of Bob, I think Badger and Shebang are in love.

> When the coyotes threatened the yard or her sanity or beagle, she answered their incantations with her own sad song, nobody knows, she'd sing. Get the hell out of dodge, she'd cry. There's a new sheriff in town. Don't come around here no more, no more, she'd say, kicking dirt.

Bob loses his tail the same day the lambs do. Sugar Daddy says to Doc, take their tails off, they'll have some personality then. Maybe they'll hunt better or fetch more money. Running Love screams, Stop. You idiot, she hollers. What the hell are you doing. She scares Doc just a little, so he puts his tail cutters back in his truck and leaves laughing. Sugar Daddy says, I'm keepin the one without a tail. I cheer, jump up and down, and take Bob for a ride in the wagon leaving Shebang and the rest of the hunters in the kennel.

> Her mistake: Old man with gun.
> Her mistake: Old man with rat poison.
> Her mistake.

Her
miss
take.

    the rat ate the hen's legs
    just the scaly part
    the part with bone and marrow
    toes and nerves
    but it was the hen's fault
    she was, after all, a broody bitch

Her unchained melody was all melancholy and magnificence.

say

Tony Orlando and Bob become the pair I know best. Tony Orlando is an Australian shepherd that looks curiously birddogish. When his breeders see what they saw when he was a pup but on a larger scale, they offer us money, they want to put the accidental dog down. There must have been a breech in the bitches vaginal security is all they can say. That ugly sorryassexcuseforadog has got to be put down, put in the ground, shot on site, shot at sight, shot in the sight, put out of mind, out of sight, out of our misery, out of their misery. Your money for his life, Sugar Daddy asks. I throw myself over the dog. I hold my breath until my throat swells almost shut and I begin to sob. To make a show of it, I vocalize. I fake a seizure, all the while, my body over Tony Orlando. Sensing the madness, Running Love hurries to my side. When she picks me up, I won't let Tony Orlando go. Running Love carries us both to the house. She is mumbling, but I don't know what she is saying. I am too busy planning an escape with Tony Orlando. Sugar Daddy chases the breeders down the road waving a large bolt cutter and kicking dirt with his size sixteen Durango boots.

        the cattle are screaming
        their babies are gone
        the cattle are screaming
        their babies are gone
          the cattle are
           screaming
         their babies
             are
            gone

Tony Orlando rides on the tank of my motorcycle, laughing at the sport. We spin round and round in the mud and circle the house. When done riding, we lie under the ash tree and talk about bullies and love and he lets me wrap my dirty arms tight around his neck. As I inhale, the scent of hound marks mind cells and places them in permanent storage. I whisper in his long tattered ear that I love him and I do. On hot summer night, I pick ticks off his head and burn them on the sidewalk with an Ohio bluetip.

> A cry baby, she whimpered songs for sorrow in the mornings until I told her that she was a good girl, my girl, my good, good girl. She wailed when she got knocked up by the neighbor's lab. It take two, baby, I told her. She didn't care.

aspIrate

> She whimpered after she ate a chick, Momma, I just killed again. She'd cry every time I left, Don't leave me this way. She cried when she delivered seven pups or when they nursed or when they grew up and moved out and she was all alone with her beagle and coyotes and coydogs again, because she was no fan of lonely days and lonely nights.

>> inside inside the words they hear, the words they think they hear, the words they think the words they hear mean, worthless, worthlesskids, worthlessbitch, worthlessbum, goodfor, goodfornothing, goodforthinngfreeloaders, worthlessgoodfornothinggoodfornothings

>> inside the baby is long gone

When the old man hit her with a stick, she cried, but cries turned to stories on the tongue of such a beautiful liar and blue notes waltzed off the tip of her slender head.

> bloody blenders
> are relieved of their contents

when dumped onto thirsty crops
or down the throat of disbelief

When she barked at the old man, her voice was all tale, O, the shark has pretty teeth, dear. All she really meant was, Leave me alone. Ain't nothin gonna break my stride.

Mr. Dirty Bas-
tard [here
today, gone to-
morrow]

D.B. of [just
down the road]
died of a heart
attack [brought
on by bitter-
ness] while
giving orders
to a blue col-
lar boob. He
enjoyed fishing
and hunting. He
worked and [we
were all sur-
prised at his
death]. He [be-
lieved he] was
well-respected.
He is survived
by [several
individuals who
appeared only
after his last
call].

I told her to stay away from the old man, but she couldn't help herself. I told her the grass was greener on our side of the world. I said, Stay home. Stay alive. She replied, Live free or die.

the cattle are lowing
their babies all gone

to kill
or not to kill

When she first disappeared, I walked for days calling her name, Hey, Jude and Maybeline and Layla, but all I could hear were the frogs chanting about love, their booty calls ringing in my ears. Every time I thought I heard her tired voice blowin in the wind, the breeze switched direction. After three days, I had a dream. When I told the search and rescue team, I had to ask them, Do you believe in magic. Yes, they answered. I dreamed a little dream and there were strawberry fields forever to the right and blueberry hill to the left. Yes, yes, the search team said. This may sound crazy, but in the still of the night, in the middle of my dream…. Tell me more. Tell me more, said a searcher. I continued, In the purple rain, just south of pasture, I dreamed she lie in the tall grass near death. Near who, asked a rescuer. Near death, I said.

to eat
or not to eat

inside glass breaks, there is spilling and running, and dangerous slivers of sharpness hiding in a shag carpet with droplets
of love   or life

When we found her she was tangled up in blue grass and stuck in a drainpipe. One end of the pipe had been crushed shut by the big tires of tractors. The other end led to the pond. She must've chased that white rabbit. She cried, her long tail making rhythms against the steel pipe. What a wonderful world.

After I leave home, Bob gets arthritis, gets snappy with the new babies, dies when his heart stops.

The old man says, come on over. He says, Be my baby.

the cattle are low
their babies all dead

DIEvorce

outside Hot Momma and Sugar Daddy go for rides to cool off, but the outside is just as hot as the inside

inside the baby is tucked away in denial

The second time she disappears, I'm struck, twisted, shaken. I am under the spell of my past or running away from a voice or confused by the traffic in my head. I'm in pieces. All the while she's dying in a ditch, a bullet in her heart, me trying to evaporate, her slowly becoming comfortably numb. I could feel her begging, Stand by me, or was it just my imagination. Miles away, I could hear crying.

He Who Shall
Remain Negative

He died of
guilt, died of
a heart con-
dition that
nobody knew.
He died while
giving hell to
a blue collar
worker who did
a poor job of
clear cutting
his woods. He
enjoyed fishing
and hunting.
He worked most
of his life in
the city not
far away. He
had one son
who visited
regularly and
several other
relatives who
had a stake in
the estate.
Most thought he
was a crazy old
bastard harbor-
ing the devil
inside. He was
a man of con-
stant sorrow.

inside I find an attic full of fun and booze it up, dance in a room full of purple and Mad Dog and rain, the smoke of cloves trailing into the shine of black light, inside I learn about glowing and growing

frI-end

Tony Orlando disappears. There is no search party, because the head searcher has moved away. For days, and then months, there is no Tony Orlando, no accidental dog to catch hunks of meat or pieces of potatoes when they are tossed in the air. Nobody to bark once at a treed raccoon. Nobody to keep the coyotes out of the yard or to cry to or to hear confessions. Forgive me. I have sinned.

>the cattle are low
>their babies are poor
>the cattle are lowing
>their poor babies done

>When I escaped my past, I crawled home, but she was not there. I lit a candle and wondered, Where oh where can my baby be. But she was not there.

Sugar Daddy finds Tony Orlando hanging in a fence, his skeleton and fur still tangled in barbed wire. There are no ticks to pull, no hound scents left, or fat neck to hold my arms. There are no flies, no worms, only bones and hide.

When I finally come home. He is not there.

>When I finally came home. She was not there.

Her Mother Who

CC imagines a mother she forgets. She feels the incantations of the mother's voice calling her through the thick underbrush of dreamscapes. Carried by a quivering undertow, the mother's songs work their way through CC's mindspaces. CC wants to reach out, wants to touch the mother's voice, wants to feel the mother's embrace but does not know where to place her arms or expectations or in which direction to face her cupped ear.

Words filter through worlds trickling in love and you and me and mine and please and baby and please. CC interrupts the words. Louder, she says. Softer, she cries. Please speak or write or hum more clearly. CC interprets words. Where, she says. Are, she cries. You, she asks. Please direct or call or (mis)lead more clearly.

What a girl wants is (not)

CC wants Louise Jefferson, Lucy Ricardo, Kitty Foreman, Mabel Thomas. She wants to remember the feel of the mother who resides only in scents of the road, only in the theory of a (mis)take, in the sound of air slipping between sorrow and celebration. CC wants to ride the allusion to its source, wants to redirect the way it travels, how it refuses to slow long enough for her to take notes.

CC tries. She lies. She cannot sleep. She sings, Where O where can she be. The notes trip over her tongue, fall from her mouth mixed with metaphors and emotions. Tongue pushing off against toothtops, she is mired down in (in) significant language. She stutters, This. That. The. There. Not what she needs. All she needs is love. Love. Love. A myth. Busted. What she does not need is

You, the voice cries, don't know what you need. CC does not (under)stand. She hears the buzz of the ball, absorbs the need, does not know why, wants to learn the language of love or of the voice or of the (m)other (figure).

You, the voice sings, don't know what you need. CC does (not) understand. She hears the melody in the sound. And the soul of not knowing. CC responds, Sing louder. Sing. Sing a song or a life or to(o) (re)direct.

She prays, Dear Mother who aren't in heaven or hell, please give me a sign. Knock three times on the ceiling or twice on the table. Spell it out in codes or send me a letter. Dear Mother, Please, she pleas. Dear. Dear. (M)other, help me (under)stand.

The voice answers. One knock and an incantation. Five taps and a murmur. Three knocks and a hum. She hears a smile in the way the knocking lilts, feels frustration in the way the murmur travels down her spine and back up toward her lips before dropping away. She reaches for a dictionary, searches for meaning and use. CC finds a fissure in the structure of the sentence. She pries it open. Begins the dialogue

Why did you

Why did you

Why did you

abandon (verb)

You the

abandon (noun)

You(')r(e) (w)reck(less)

abandon (noun)

Why (adverb + interjection + noun) (a simultaneous mix of states of be(ginn)ing

be what(ever)

you be(come)

Her (m)other (it) figure's best advice, slicing through the dank exterior of a fading language (or body or self imag(i)e(d))

barrier.

We are making progress, growing and developing. Movin on up.

Through darkness, tangled in briars, shoes weighed down by clay.

CC imagines a mother she forgets. She feels the incantations of the mother's voice calling her through the thick underbrush of dreamscapes. Carried by a quivering undertow, the mother's songs work their way through CC's mindspaces. CC wants to reach out, wants to touch the mother's misty voice, wants to feel the mother's embrace but does not know where to place her arms or expectations or in which direction to face her cupped ear.

Words filter through worlds trickling in love and words like you and me and mine

MAD WORLD

faces of strangers, faces of friends, of foes close in, pass through her, featureless orbs in orbit, then nothing, then in orbit again—epigraph

she dreams herself in a short   red car   rims metallic in the sun rolling backwards the scene rushing forward to the sounds of lynard skynard as yellowgray dashlines connect   this baby can handle a turn   baby can handle   a turn   baby can she reaches a flat-a-way the odometer can't keep up   she keeps rolling and rushing into a tree or telephone pole or brick building   her head pressed against broken glass   blood spilling or only dripping onto the pavement or in the crown vetch lined ditch trickling into the open mouths of lilies

she dreams herself wrapped in the arms of a harness   atop a tree matted cliff or atop a needled tree   an eagle passing above or she is the eagle   the scent of pine musk of a fox smack of the river floating up as she rushes toward the water and snaps back to be near or to be the eagle then down and to the clifftop the hardrock side and little survivor trees a blur and back down and a snap but this time she's swimming toward the blue but not of the sky she is swimming so fast that the sounds of the voices blur and smack against her skull

she dreams herself in a business suit and pencil skirt in a suite tapping a laptop calling home to two daughters   blonde curls around pink faces   and a steroid enhanced rugged unshaven husband and they love her and miss her already and the husband laughs that they should find or have more children and she can tell she can smell something in the background at the backside of the screen   an uneasy presence   she can taste sulfur in the thundersounds   and she says the words love and miss and soon and love and there is a silence the humidity of sin frizzing the curls   staining the blonde

never having dreamed

                                        never trusting a dream
                                          she doesn't dream
                                      doesn't believe in dreams

she dreams herself a rock queen on a rock stage   pyrotechnics exploding behind
her to every side surrounding her in sparkling flames and fumes   she's a caged
tiger   pawing out reaching toward the sea of clawing hands and featurefree
orbs   when she reaches closer they lung forward   foreign and familiar
the stage caves in   fading flames lighting up glints of metal   glimpses of
smoking synthetics snapshots of nothing   before she feels the weight of some
thing pressing against her breast tightening with the exhale moving in closer
deeper   deeper
              deeper

she dreams herself   facedown sunblasted in a desert   an oasis swimming yards
away her limp legs twist backwards her arms crossed across her chest beneath
her holding a rose or cactus or lucky hare's foot   the oasis crowd is
wild   stigmas and stamen swaying   she sees the curves of their bodies dancing
or loving or convulsing in death   the long waves of their hair   their faces
sunbright and indistinguishable they gaze at her with empty sockets and continue
to groove and grind on heatwaves   drinking umbrellaed glasses of blue
the oasis floating away

                                        never having dreamed
                                          she doesn't dream
                                        doesn't trust dreams

TRICKLE DOWN

how his hands became
weapons how de
sire swam up a stream or
dream of love twisting in
to fire and rage
and shame   and

how his will pried her
open   splitting   her
at the
                        soul
separating atrium from
              ventricle (only a
feeling)   (hooked on a
feeling)

how tears
blocked by
his story   blocked
by hystery blocked
by in   jury backed
into throat and
stomach and   mind
and

how blame circled   how a
predator biting at
sorrow   biting at her
self (missed) per
                    ception
teeth tearing away
                    at time

how guilt f   lowed
between them cementing
hidden tales   each
crack fixed
                    by shame

how his desire
            became hers

how resistance
            became his

how their shame
                spun and
                severed or stirred
                                tiny
circles

SEX STORIES

Story 1: There is a girl who says things like No and Please and Don't and Stop and Leave and Me and Alone.

Story 2: She passes, cuts through air and time, avoiding. Her scent climbs rising heat, advancing up bodies. A little bit and more. Her breath working around space as if it doesn't want. But it does. Something. Wants some thing. Her hair wraps loose. Her neck. Her face. And that curve. It always comes back to how that curve moves. And desires. And conforms. How it reaches out toward space before falling away.

Story 3: A virgin slut with the pigtails low, ponytail high, with lemon juice and peroxide, with Clairol and big dreams or disillusions or mistakes waiting, wading in sorrow.

Story 4: Language is born between clicks and vowels.

Story 5: There is really no such thing as sex.

Story 6: It comes down to this. It comes down to the cock. Comes down to how it crows. How loud it celebrates mo(u)rning.

Story 7: Baby goes all the way to the *Rolling Stone*. Tasting ink, melting text. She compares (im)perfection to im(perfection) and wins. She feels good vibrations but cannot hear the call. Lust, her lover tries to say. Words caught between passion and regret. The lover says nothing, doesn't want to know what's in the shadows but keeps looking. I can't help it, says the lover. Baby goes all the way on the cover of the *Rolling Stone*, cannot speak with words, uses imagery to do things. To do everything. Almost everything.

Story 8: Beverly Hills Boy has a sporty, rusted car. He moves fast, produces that laugh thick with the scent of XXX, growing. A vineyard full of sensations, growing ripe in the sun, bursting. She wants to take him home and keep him but cannot remember where home is. He asks if she parties all the time. She thinks not. Never. Hardly ever, she means. She reaches for him, but he's rolling away.

Stop, she says. Stop. His ride roars, shoving her desires aside. He is headed toward Malibu Mansion or Somewhere Exotic, a space she cannot imagine, cannot read. Come back, she says. The road rock dust rolls in on itself. There are too many clouds to know whether the sun is setting or rising.

Story 9: Before Bob Barker wants your pet spayed or neutered, there are dogs having puppies because that's what dogs do. A bitch has a litter of fourteen little brown coydogs, canines that will never make a pet, that will surely terrorize livestock and children. Thirteen of the puppies are tossed into a burlap sack and taken to the river where they float and sink, whine and weep, swallow liquid death and resurface, catfish biting on burlap until the sack comes undone and the bodies free to sink or wash up and decay. The fourteenth puppy is kept as an experiment. As a pup it tries to have sex with legs, furniture, a goat, and a coyote before being castrated with a hunting knife.

Story 10: There is a girl. A really bad girl. She swears. And swears to gods. And, because she is a really bad girl, she has sex. A lot of sex. This makes her bad. Makes her a worse girl than the girl she was when she only swore. There is always a bad girl having sex so the good girls can feel better about their re/depression.

Story 11: How his hands become
                weapons. How desire swims
up   the stream of love twisting into fire
                             and rage and shame and

How his will pries her open,   splits her at the soul. Separ   ating.

Story 12: An 18-year-old man is charged with raping a 5-month-old baby girl while her mother is in class at the local high school. The baby (who requires surgery and cries hard enough to either vomit or overfill her lungs with melancholy) might have been crying too loud for the man to tolerate or the man might have been on drugs or drunk or the baby might have been asking for it or the man might have just needed to satisfy an urge. Fifty years earlier, a mother castrates her newborn son. The infant's screaming or the shame of having a disfigured child or the understanding of the possible spiritual or legal consequences is too much. A century earlier a father rapes a 10-month-old daughter who bleeds to death and is placed (along with several rocks and flowers) in a burlap sack and sent to the bottom of a river that flows into the Mississippi and then into the Gulf of Mexico. It is unclear how far the body, bricks, burlap, or flowers travel before being consumed by fish or mud.

Story 13: There's a baby in a basket on a fence post down a country road, a crow on her head, geese beneath her post. She's flashing through the weave and nobody knows. Nobody cares. Nobody understands. Without stimuli, the baby cries and sings.

HERSTORY

Waking me, a dictionary or bible or work boot slams against my chest. This is what it feels like to be shot or to have a heart attack. This is what it feels like when you roll a tractor or land beneath a building or when a cat suffocates a baby.

A gunshot echoes through my skull, slapping against my head smacking like a gong. This is what it sounds like to be shot or to step on a bomb. This is what it sounds like to have your head pried open by a crowbar or ball bat or train tire.

The voices repeat, What's wrong with you. And, Please, baby. Please. And, Everybody loves a good girl. The voices swear and swear to gods.

At midnight, beneath my window, the
goose honks.

What, I ask.

He honks.

I get up, throw a tomato at him, go
back to bed.

He honks again.

What, I say.

Honk.

I go outside, fill the pool.

The dogs pounce on me with filthy
feet; they knock me senseless into mud,
stick burs in my hair, and stamp me
with skunk scent.

this
is
what
it
feels
like
to
be
wanted

Jane L. Carman

The cops come to say, These dogs bark too
much. We have a complaint. The cops stay
in their car and point at each dog.

They don't bark enough, I say.

They can't bark at night, they say. There are
too many.

I say, Too many dogs or too many barks.

Both, they say.

These two don't bark, I say, pointing at the
bird dogs. I'll tell the others.

It doesn't matter, they say. Control your
dogs. The dogs can only travel as far as the
edge of the ditch, they say, pointing at the
side nearest the house.

I say, Can I make a complaint.

Sure, they say.

Can you please keep the coyotes quiet, I say.
A raccoon ate the best hen last night, could
you please arrest it. The raccoon, I add. It's
too late for the hen.

They laugh and begin to pull away.

Is it not funny how the hen died. She was
alive when they started eating, I say. These
aren't my dogs, anyway.

Who do they belong to, they wander.

I don't know, I say. They came here on their
own.

You feed them, they say.

I say, Yes, but I don't clean up their shit. I'd
feed you, if you were hungry. And nicer.

They say
things
like, They
are yours.
And,
Keep
them
quiet.
And,
Make sure
they don't
go past
that ditch.

I

too

say

things.

The frogs
are having a
ball.
Catcalling
and
hissing.

For two
months, they
roll the dark
night air into
staccato,
stretto, and
vibrato.

A crop duster
sprays a
neighboring
field. Fog
floats on a
wet wave of
air into the
windows.

The cats
heave.

The dogs
won't eat.

The goose
honks.
Invisible
particles hide
in the eggs.

At two in the
morning, a
helicopter
drags over
the house.

As I open
my eyes,
they are
filled with
spackling
and a spider
shaken loose
from above.

I stick my
head in the
shower and
this time
I swear
to place a
sign in the
sky, right
next to that
worthless
spirit.

When I trip
over her, the
cat looks at
me.

She narrows
her eyes and
stands by the
door.

I open it and
she leaves,
twitching her
tail.

Purring, the
cat sleeps
on my legs.

I am
trapped.
I can't
roll, can't
rearrange.
My knees
flinch.

The cat
wails and
treads
across my
face.

Don't tread,
I say. I rest
my hot head
against cool
sheets.

Feral
thoughts
tear away in
a billowing,
bellowing
fog.

A little gray car full of little gray men in sensible suits pulls into the drive. They sit and press on the horn.

The goose honks back.

The dogs bark and circle the car.

Sickem, I say.

Honk.

Honk.

They glare at me. Hold up a paper.

I walk to the window, say, Sickem.

The dogs jump up scratching the paint, reaching into the cracked window.

Can you call your dogs off, they say.

I could, I say. But they aren't mine.

Would you be interested, they say.

No, I say.

The dogs are pissing on tires.

You don't know why we are here, they say.

I'm not interested, I say. Get off my property.

They drive away, a dog hanging onto the glass until it reaches that line across the ditch; when it gets there it drops and rolls.

At night,
the
clothes
rack
rustles,
metal
grazing
against
metal,
the hard
fabric of
coats
grating
across
overalls.

Shhhh, I say. Be quiet, I say. Stop it, I say. Then, silence. I remind myself to put a sign on the clothes rack and one on my heavy head.

A little rusty car approaches the barking
pack. I wait for a horn. There's a whirl
of canine refrains and reproaches

A boy exits the car.

My rifle and I approach.

Not noticing my friends, he begins his
speech, I am selling children's books to
pay my way through college.

The dogs continue to circle in semi-
silence.

Do I look like a child, I say.

No, he says.

The goose approaches, Honk.

Do I look like someone who reads
kiddie books, I say.

Yes, he says. No.

No, I say.

They ate the last salesman, I say.

He smiles.

Honk. Honk, honk.

Killed him dead, I say.

He laughs.

Ate him alive, I say. One little word and
they'll eat you.

What would that word be, he says.

If I tell you, they'll hear, I say. Then
I'll have to hide your little car and burn
those books.

At night
the door
knobs rattle,
starting at the
southwest
corner and
working their
way
around the
house. Each
knob jingles
for seven
seconds.

There is a beat
and bang on
my bedroom
window.

I throw a tin
bandage box
toward the
sound,
splintering
glass into a
spider.

The dogs
wake up and
begin barking,
leaping
toward
the
pain.

Would you be, he begins.

No, I say. What's wrong with you.
Aren't you scared of dogs.

No, he says.

awkward

space

between

us

We have some interesting nature books,
he says, quickly.

I hate nature, I say.

Petting a dog, he begins, I'm sure we
have something.

I stop him. Listen, I say, you have to
leave now.

Do you know anyone with children, he
asks.

Hate kids, I say.

But you know someone.

Are you that desperate, I say looking at
the trigger of my rifle.

Yes, he says.

Maybe a mile down the road and a mile
up the road, I say. Now get.

Thanks, he says with his arm around
the former best dog.

There is
a ringing
in the air,
something
menacing,
mechanical.
It passes
through my
left lobe,
pauses
behind my
eyes, and
circles my
brainstem
before
moving
out.

Ring and
rang and
rung.

I post a
mental
sign.

I tow the
kitchen table
across the
room and
out the front
door.

Dogs pushing
footpads into
my spine, the
goose
honking, I
drag it down
the drive
toward that
line in the
ditch.

I set the table
in the gravel,
spray paint the
top, No
Trespassing,
in big white
letters pulsing
against the
mahogany.

I turn the
sign to one
side and
block the
entrance.

By morning, the table top is clean. It looms in the kitchen with a plate of cold bacon on it.

I remind myself to put a sign on my sign.

As I begin to draw it back out that ringing returns. It overtakes my brain settling into the valleys of gray matter, forcing them open. I see now there is a dead dog on the sofa and one in the shower, a pile of kiddie books in the sink. A note sprayed onto the floor. The scent of decay fills the air, seeps down my throat. This is what death tastes like. This is what it tastes like to be slapped in the face with roadkill or to eat bad meat. This is what it smells like in a packing plant or coffin.

I push against the table, but it won't budge. I call for the best dog, but she's not there. I call for the goose, but she's gone. That cat never came back. I drag the two dead bodies past that line by the ditch—on the table, I wait.

ere is honking and barking and silence.
ere is barking and honking and silence.
ere is silence and barking and honking.
ere is honking and barking and silence.
ere is barking and honking and silence.
ere is silence and barking and honking.
ere is honking and barking and silence.
ere is barking and honking and silence.
ere is silence and barking and honking.
ere is honking and barking and silence.
ere is barking and honking and silence.
ere is silence and barking and honking.
ere is honking and barking and silence.
ere is barking and honking and silence.
ere is silence and barking and honking.
ere is honking and barking and silence.
ere is barking and honking and silence.
ere is silence and barking and honking.
ere is honking and barking and silence.
ere is barking and honking and silence.
ere is silence and barking and honking.
ere is honking and barking and silence.
ere is barking and honking and silence.
ere is silence and barking and honking.
ere is honking and barking and silence.
ere is barking and honking and silence.
ere is silence and barking and honking.
here is honking and barking and silence.
here is barking and honking and silence.

Nobody knows how clean I peal a po
Nobody knows how good I am at being a wo
Nobody knows how well I play g
Nobody knows how clean I peal a po
Nobody knows how good I am at being a wo
Nobody knows how well I play g
Nobody knows how clean I peal a po
Nobody knows how good I am at being a wo
Nobody knows how well I play g
Nobody knows how clean I peal a po
Nobody knows how good I am at being a wo
Nobody knows how well I play g
Nobody knows how clean I peal a po
Nobody knows how good I am at being a wo
Nobody knows how well I play g
Nobody knows how clean I peal a po
Nobody knows how good I am at being a wo
Nobody knows how well I play g
Nobody knows how clean I peal a po
Nobody knows how good I am at being a wo
Nobody knows how well I play g
Nobody knows how clean I peal a po
Nobody knows how good I am at being a wo
Nobody knows how well I play g
Nobody knows how clean I peal a po
Nobody knows how good I am at being a wo
Nobody knows how well I play g
Nobody knows how clean I peal a po
Nobody knows how good I am at being a wo
Nobody knows how well I play g
Nobody knows how clean I peal a po

For the Love of the Storyteller

From the time she was first swaddled and swallowed by his cracked hands, holding her against his chest, she was his, a Daddy's daughter, a love of(f) the old block, a growing bundle of (in)justice, (com)passion, fight, and danger.

At the age of seven, he placed his palm in the cool wet concrete of a new well and said, "Now, when your old dad dies, you can come here and see my hand." In that moment, sun and uncertainty washing over her, the child understood fragility and mortality, understood there were invisible cracks in the hero's sun-brown exterior, cracks that, from that moment on, she worked to discover and mend.

She believed that, if she never left his side, he could not die. If she could always see him as a man, there would be no need to go back to the handprint. She followed him from barnyard to field tossing flakes of hay to horses and mules, riding on the rusty orange fender of the old tractor, looking first off into the fields then at the creases growing deep and soft around his eyes, looking at the wiry white blow of hair that had long ago surrendered color for the flush of wisdom. She stood behind gates watching him cultivate wild horses, wishing she were the one riding and he the one marveling.

His love was passion filled with violence and language informed by the pedagogy of hardness, of labor and love and loss. He was compassion riding a beast into the sunset. He was love leaving meat for a coyote tripping through a frozen field. He was power spinning fabulous tales, twisting experience into song, lore into legend.

She watched his stories grow, watched the men gather round drinking bottles of soda, laughing, sparkling nearly as bright as a gold tooth. She watched his audience consume tales letting the words slide past doubt, move past reality and desire where they'd take up residence in the mindspaces of those who'd respin his language into (dis)belief or admiration or hate or love or desire.

It was too much, that love. That responsibility to want to keep him close, so close she could not breathe, she could not move, so close she could not live. When she pushed herself outside of his charmed utterances, she collapsed and moved back toward him, toward his magnetic soul. She circled and spun, moving in closer and closer as time began to threaten her world, his fantastic life, his epic, their tragedy.

She cried and pulled and dug her soul into the earth. Her passion exploded against each diagnosis, against each movement he made toward his finale. His passion moved inward, as he could no longer punch or kick or move away from the edge. In his eyes, she could see the words begin to form. Those eyes no longer held beautifully spun adventures; they begged for time, for help, for peace. They wanted to remain or redeem, to hang on and out, to be and be and be. But they could not.

So distraught over what she could not accept, she moved against the inevitable pushing for a reversal of circumstances or health or time, begging the doctors to do something, to do anything, to do and do and do and keep doing. But the doctors failed.

Every day for as long as she could remember, she feared his death, devoted her life to his, acted toward the impossible project of keeping that father alive for ever and for her (his daughter). Her desire to extend his life increasing as he began his descent; she labored toward that impossible goal, toward the denial of a final movement. A refusal of any final moment.

In the end, she failed to keep that body moving on and

away, to save him from his biggest fear.

She returns to the well, to the handprint, studies the creases in the fingers. They were deeper than she remembers. Time works against the concrete, against his want for her to visit the old dad's handprint, but nothing can keep down her desire to reconstruct the past, to craft and renew and relive the days of a dusty girl riding in a field or pasture or leaning against the chest pocket of a pair of faded bibs to listen to the rhythm of the story teller's heart.

What O What Can We Be

It seems I am not myself, she says.
I am neither myself nor yourself, she says.
How might we begin to become ourselves.
By trending in the might direction.
By moving north or beast.
By breaking in the correct coordinates.
It seems I am experiencing a slippage of self.
My brain is beginning to slide.
Our movements are being moderated.
Our moderations are beginning movements.
My bane is beginning to ride.
My main is sliding to a cry.
Our cries move us south of ourselves.
Our selves aren't those we imagined.
What did we perceive.
What did we miss.
Our histories are high from smoking our fissures.
We are exposed by our steamy fixations.
I am not, she says.
Myself, she says.
We are not, she says.
Ours, she says.

o
baby
0 baby
whatever
happened to
baby to the baby
to the baby by the
river or the baby hiding
in a dark hot cavern the baby
with two legs or with four legs or
the one-legged baby and the baby who
never grew her legs who never ran away
from that boy with fat wet lips and a hard
zipper or who never ran away from that man
with a gun or knife or loaf of bread   the one who
couldn't give chase because he tripped over his own ego
or because his hair was tongue-tied to an elm or bedpost
or because he pecked at a keyboard so long he forgot how
to run or move or use the language of (pick a poison) or because
he was never a man because he was a crow all along surfing on the
back of a baby toeing her storyline until he dropped away in a mess of
multiple-syllabled chants or because he was really a duck   (pick a vowel)
or a duck (pick a consonant) or most likely a goose spinning the tale of a little
orphaned babe or baby or a maybe with black or red or white or blue and gray skin
sparkling hot against the set of a sun being chewed by amber waves of pain or purple
anger grainy with (dis)allusions of time and illness (sick bastards swimming against the
pride) slicing through brown-red clay tossing the artifacts of grandmothers holding great
and greats in their dusty hands that tapped rock against rock rolling that clay into shape and
tool and cup that fed old babies dead for decades or centuries or for no reason other than gender
or appearance or lack of lack of caused by hunger or greed or an inability to snare that which sustains
or detains or dies waiting for sorrow to trickle down through the hands of sands or time not knowing love

knowing lore and lust bearing bsby babies into killing and dying times or times where baby baby daze is like

two sides of a battle   good winning evil winning good being evil being good being tangled in a web of sanity

or wanting somemority or lessity or fishy tiny lungs filling with green water or waves of tenderness cast by

mothers wanting to spare a life wanting to spare struggle or pain for the self or the other or the selfish

others who lies beneath a cover of brambles or the rumbling darkness of a shadowy storm bringing

language and monster to life to live on the slim branches of a lightning-struck tree so deep

in denial that it cannot escape the shadow it casts upon babes and babies and mothers

treading the thick blood of slippery slopes designed to funnel these little lives

those little lies into the belly of a hungry mother into the belly of a hungry

monster into the belly of a swallowing hole that digests and rejects

sending bones and souls screaming or dreaming or lost toward the

surface of a field or dream or skimming the edge of a prayer

or desperate act intended to please a Him or a him or to

disguise an act rendered senseless or useless or worth

less on a scale ranking from one to him or from

fine to not or from virgin to horror from

whore to more to more and more

an old woman drinking horror

living and breathing that

which is forbidden as

language forbodden

as reality forbidden

as narrative as life

as reality as

being any

thing

not

hi

n

g

(S)P(L)ACE

I sit curled next to Running Love, her lilac perfume as clear as spring, as strong as the shrubs growing in her garden. It is Sunday night. We watch *Wild Kingdom*, *Lawrence Welk*, *Disney*. Regardless of age or circumstance, she calls me a hotten tot or cherub.

I am in Sweet Daddy's gaze as I deliver a slick blackblue lamb, its steaming body sliding into the cold February air, its mother cleaning. I am in his gaze as I learn to drive a rusty International. I cut it too sharp, tearing open a tire with the grain wagon, the moist, rubbery air whooshing by my face; as I climb down. Sweet Daddy observes in silence.

I'm watching Hot Momma melt away between her desire to satisfy Sugar Daddy's needs for love and profit and her inability to embrace the idea that where there is livestock there is deadstock, that the bottle lambs she feeds either become roasts or burdens, that when the dog she talks to every day is hit by a truck the only option is death, that when the dog dies there's a new one the next day to learn his work, because farms never rest.

I walk the hard, black soil in the wake of gleaming disks picking up ancient pottery that never fits together, collecting arrowheads and axes, holding the old black pipe still bearing the mark of gut or vine that once connected it to the rest of history. I clutch the paintrock, rub it across my cheeks, the iron coloring my skin. I'm listening to Sweet Daddy's stories of ancestors—his longing for something primordial, something he cannot touch.

I hear the pheasant's cry, high and harsh, beneath the brown and red of winter scrub. I see a merry-go-round of vultures, circling just out of reach, past the pond that shrinks out of existence when the sky refuses to weep—the same pond where, in wetter years, frogs chorus rounds of love songs between spring rain and snow showers—the most determined pairs of balled eyes poking out of water puddles surrounded by moats of snow.

I'm warning the roosters not to crow at midnight, not to crow at 2:00 a.m. I tell the ducks not to shit on the steps. The roosters run away, chasing a hen. Under the dogs' protection, the ducks' laughter is unmistakable. They laugh at me. They laugh at night, at opossums and raccoons. The taunting voices that refuse to res(is)t.

I plant domestic rudbeckia and echinacea, their supermodel improvements making them stand out against their pallid ancestors in the same way my muted skin contrasts that of Sweet Daddy, of Running Love, of their ancestors. The

flowers grow in purple and gold ovals,
creating new boundaries each season

I am in the living room. Outside the
window, Leopold's crane passes yearly.
I watch the hawk fly by, carrying a
writhing snake like Indiana Jones,
snapping a whip. The returning eagle
clutches a screaming rabbit. Running
Love teaches me names/identities,
behaviors, reminds me of the math
that divides and multiplies and
subtracts these species.

I search but cannot find a prairie dog,
buffalo, or porcupine.

Feral cats and rabbits are addition.
Addition equals subtraction.

The crop dusters miss fields sprinkling
houses, ponds, and pets. The cat comes
home, head on sideways, mewing,
aborting her kittens. Stumbling, she
does not die. A friend dies from
cancer. Running Love's children die
from cancer. Sweet Daddy refuses to
speak of the reason he walks bent,
rubs his stomach, eats less. Sugar
Daddy goes to clinics, shrinks and
recovers. A cat dies from cancer, then
a goat and a horse. People die for
reasons. For other reasons. The voices
die, are reborn; they morph and taunt.
When I speak, I ask them for peace or
silence. They will not listen.

I watch a coyote down a rifle barrel
and decide whether or not to pull
the trigger. I don't fire. I kill seven

watersnakes, two opossums, five snapping turtles and a raccoon with a pellet gun to protect rabbits, chickens, ducks, and cats. A battle between indigenous and domestic. I don't know how to stand atop this fence. I am out of balance.

I need to find awe in less space than Thoreau. This is not a choice.

Soldiers die from things like shrapnel, neglect, (mis)communication, greed. For several years, war plan(e)s and helicopters have purred through the night air indifferent to this place. Night after month after year, I've listened for silence but cannot hear it for the howling, crowing, humming, screaming, buzzing.

SHE SAYS

It's hotter than a three-peckered billy goat on the fourth of July,
she says.
It is close, she says.
Close to what, she wanders.
The corn is tasseling toward gaudiness.
The flash of summer is messing with my missing.
It is hot, she says. Hot.
It is July and the corn is past the top of the headstone.
Knee high, she says.
By the force of July, she says.
He isn't worth a pecker's damn, she says.
Tarnations, she says.
His ass is grass, she says.
I'm a lawn mower, she says.
Messing is moving with my inhibitions.
She is canning tomatoes and green beans. She is preserving ber-
ries and apples.
She is preserving language, history, a child.
My can is degenerating poetry.
Apples perversed by the pressure of the cooker.
She defies time with glass jars.
She defies thyme with reciprocal measures.
I am sustaining, she says.
Mantaining, she says.
She wears housedresses.
Horseflies depressing my loneliness.
A saddle on a sow, she says.
She is saving her legs.
Shave the eggs, she says.
How many bakers in a dozen.
Dozers shifting away the thyme.
Speak the truth, she says.
Dozers filling in ponds.
Shame the devil, she says.

Mud burying the frogs so deep that their music cannot be heard.
Shame, she says.
He has none, she says.
Shame that is.
Same that is.
I took it all, she says.
Shame, shame, shame. Tsk, tsk, tsk.
Not tea, she says.
Temptation teasing away my shame.
Nothing, she says.
Mining delineating my resources.
A man's work, she says.
She sings about sunup and sundown.
A woman's work, she says.
Never done.
Never gone.
A woman's work defines the woman.
She is defied by her work.
As a woman, she says. I am never.
Iskibble, she says.
She is color.
Damn the color, she says.
Shame on this color, she says.
She is wearing the sun, scrubbing away history.
She is not partly. Not party.
A woman's work, she cries.
Her color fakes into voice.
Her voice returns to color.
She is messing.
Missing.
Mine.

REPRISE: THE ROAD

CC returns to the road
where geese (w)rapped around post
where the ghost of a mosaic haunts the earth
where the trace of a plastic laundry basket begins to break
down

CC returns to the still road
tasting her tears
her blood
turning her sorrow into stone
her innocence into marrow

CC returns to the still gravel road
her spirit searching for Motorcycle Momma
her eyes for crow or goose
her heart for Hot Momma's loss, Sugar Daddy's lost, Sweet
Daddy's love
her body probing for tigers and frogs
her hands for course, soft cattails

CC returns to the still gravel road holding
the center of her life
       fading
              wasting
                      blanking
                             searching
                                    irreplaceable

CC returns to the still gravel road grasping actions
she cannot (re)call
cannot taste how the dust feels in her
how the downy, slick geese brushed against her future memories
how the nails of a crow dug through her scalp
how it messed her hair, her back, her

how the powdery stamen of lilies yellowed her caress
how the road continues to reach out toward the good vibrations
of faded mother(s)

CC returns to the still gravel road building her tension
cradling beginnings
(mis)shapping endings
treasuring square inches and miles and millimeters of scored baby
longing for baby, baby days
willing (hi)story and long locks to flow backward into
waiting for the return of lilies and cattails and geese and frogs and
reaching out for loss and lost and love and
yearning for that which can never be

FINALE

She's standing in a cornfield thinking about how she got there. Girls surround her creating a grid of long hair flowing backwards, reaching away from despair, driving toward a depression. They think about what they are. Why. There. In the corn. In the field. On pedestals. Feet vanishing into blades. Tassels decorating or aggravating their ankles. They might move away from the scene but don't. Or cannot. Still against their little dresses. Transparent, their shirts fail to reach as fair as long strands of wheat or black or white hair. Waving little banners. Advertising youth or beauty or something packaged in desire.

They are response.

She's tangled at a post. On a column in a cornfield thinking about how she arrived. Almost women box her in, long strands bursting from her skull push against her stillness. She wonders if she is paralyzed. The plant tops tickle her ankles. Feeling the ripple of a pilomotor reflex working its way up her legs, caressing her calves, traveling up toward her thighs, she stops. Thinking. She is trinket. Is trivia. Trivial. She is

Force. She refocuses. Reflects on her forefathers. Wealth. Poverty. Apparition. Voice. She refocuses. Recalls the downy embrace of her childhood. She stops. The piloerections moves toward the white of a cloud. Causes discomfort that she welcomes with the hum of vowels.

She's staging on a post. Atop a cornfield. She is surrounded by images of her self. From a distance they look like magic. Like they are rising from the earth,

a crescendo of waves born of neatly lined curves.

She thinks about her foremothers. A madwoman. A woman wrapped in sorrow. Love. Sound. Her soul wanders amongst the girls who appear younger and more than her. Who appear older than she imagines herself. Her mind wanders. He body will not follow. She thinks she is paralyzed but does not try to move. She tries to sing. Or cry. Tries to raise her voice toward the gray of that which hovers or soars.

She is floating on a corn field. She is alone. She is not   a

She is hanging over a field. Hair flowing backwards. Thinking about
                                                        Thinking that

Wonders and wanders. Wheat and black and white waving on wind, waving at

She is

From atop her post, she can see miles or centuries or the tops of things she does not understand. She can see love

loss

lost. She does not know why. She is waiting. Can not move. Or is it will not. She wants to know if she is paralyzed. She lea(r)ns.

As she falls, voices call. She is ready, they say. To be, the say. P(r)icked.

As she descends through language and time or the concreteness of the crop, voices call. She is ready, they say. For, they say. The plucking. They say, or

Wheat and black and white wrap and rap against

Big arms scoop her up. Place her back in the position. She pretends. Faints. Rolling to the side, she lands with her head in the loam. She tastes ancestral blood or loathing. She hears herds and footsteps and the building or death of a nation or girl or something she cannot understand. But she

She is at or on the podium, thinking about how she got there. The grid of girls grow their hair backwards. Glowing. Longing. Touching the next in line. They are aging. Cannot become women or older. Cannot become voices or apparitions. They might be violence or o/de/re/pression. They are dappled shadows over the field below, tassels crisping in the sun. Green blades rusting. She believes. She is paralyzed. She wants

wants to

> The sun tanning her in square inches
> and miles. Taking

her
back.

She pretends to faint. Rolls off, landing face in the mud. She tastes fear and love. She tastes battles, but cannot lick war. She is drowning in something. Maybe it is tomorrow. She is stuck. Thinking about why she cannot move. How she got there. Stuck in a fault. Lined up in the loamy, lonely mud.

Voices sing, She is. They sing, She is ready. They sing, to be. Come.

Big arms scoop her up, place her on a stand. She looks, she thinks. She tastes the air for something new. Remembers love. Is fore. Thinks about play. The girls or women. Is there red in the wheat, she wonders. Dasler bumps. Harassing her arms. Her neck. Her resistance. Her. She stops. Thinks about what's behind her. Or in front. What has she past? She needs to know. But cannot. Think. A bout. She has to move on or over or up. Maybe back. So she pretends. Falls. She misses. The field. She misses. The air. She misses. Is spinning free. A crow flies high above her. A symbol of something she cannot remember. She is reflex. Standing on end. On guard. All defense and stimulus.

There are no big arms. No pick up.

She is swimming through amber waves of pain.

She tastes uncertainty or something new. She licks the air for voices,

cannot pick up their s(c)ent. Forgets about

love and
                    sheerness. Spots a rol

                                        ling funnel on a grave

                                                            l road and re

members the pleasure of a d

                            itch full of lilies. B

                                                    urning ticks off a dog that
smells like lanolin and

death.   Riding in a pick

up or on a pony that feels as big as a horse. Sin

                                            ging on high in a field of c

        lover. She is not paralyzed. She s

lips past thin

king, moves toward that f

                        eeling, toward the beg

                                        in

                                                    ning of a

new

narrative,

one where the fal

l

in

g action l

and

s on so

ft syll

ables.

REVISION

There is a no baby.

There is no a fencepost holding a baby above a black and blue eggshell mosaic over dust and clover. Over being over.

The baby that is not a metallic light baby refuses to glow over a Sweet or Sugar Daddy over a Motorcycle or Hot Momma. Over a Beautiful Mother or Running Love desiring deep in distress. Over love and loss and lost.

There is a no baby no longer a baby.

Baby baby days are over. Dog days over.

There is no life built on voices, centered on the beginning or end of (a way of) life, centered on sex and sexuality, dreaming of daze where time fills with tongues and dreams and sincere reality, where realism drops away, trickling down a leaf or song or river, fading into the rolling dust of a rocking road.

There is no fact, no memory settling on thyme, carried away by bees and the humming of

Lullaby away. Lullababy.

There is no conclusion. No final paragraph. Return to a story. Recount dance steps. Quick, quick, slow. Click, click, bang.

A show.

Pick a consonant or vowel or constant sorrow.

You have tasted her breath and it feels like

CPSIA information can be obtained at www.ICGtesting.com
Printed in the USA
BVOW08s2016220415

397294BV00044B/786/P